# Family cheater

*(Cheating beyond expectations)*

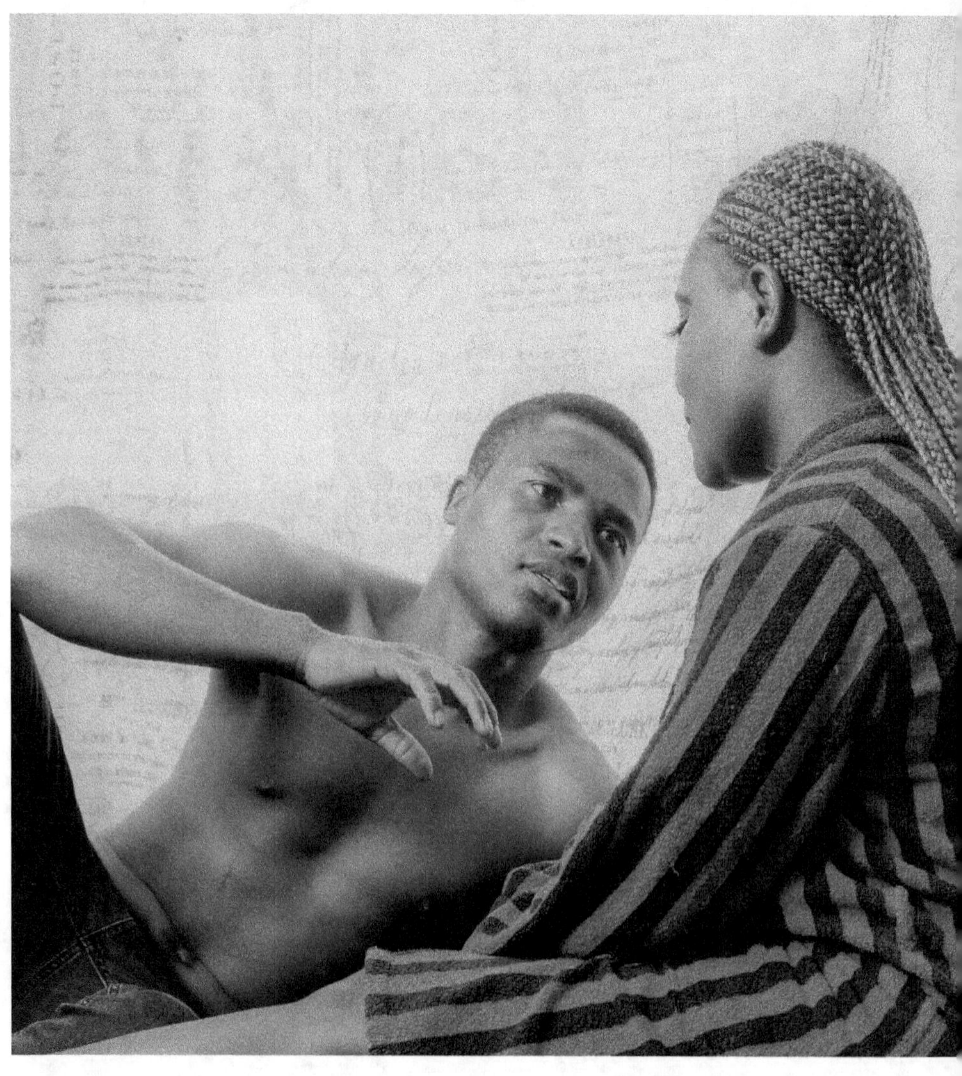

Writer: Malogwa Mutshidzi     Editor: Raphunga Ndamulelo

Mutshinya Orifha Simon

# About the author

Malogwa Mutshidzi is a South African citizen who was born in 1995. He grew up in ponderous situation; this is because he was born in a poor family. He was raised by his grandmother because his mother left him when he was still very young. He passed his matric in 2016 then he became ambitious, and he wrote plenty of books. The books were sent to Pearson publisher for educational purpose.

## Dedication

This book is dedicated to those people that are in relationships, marriages etc.

## Declaration

Malogwa Mutshidzi declares that a book called Family Cheater belongs to him,' He didn't copy it elsewhere.

## Acknowledgement

I would like to thank my friends Raphunga Ndamulelo and Mutshinya Orifha Simon for convincing me and showing me that anything is possible. They also helped edit this book.

My sincere gratitude goes to Muavhelo Takalani who took beautiful pictures for the cover page of this book.

I would also like to thank Tshivhi Elelwani for agreeing to take those pictures.

# Chapter 1

"I am really sorry for my eccentrically night; it's just like we can't be having sex each and every night we go to bed"

"We haven't been having sex for about three weeks Elisha! It's outrageous towards me now, I'm beginning to have a lot of confusion in my mind, because it seems like you're trying to manipulate me"

"It's not like that, Terry! I know we must have sex since we are married! But it shouldn't be like we are possessed with sex!"

"It seems like you are having fornication with someone out there……"

"What do you mean Terry? You think I'm……."

Terry says this and goes straight to the bedroom, he seems traumatic.

The controversy between Terry Denson and his wife Elisha is happening while they're in the kitchen. Elisha is busy preparing the feast for her husband and her little daughter while wearing lingerie and a crop top. It seems like Elisha is having lack of libido for her husband Terry Denson.

Elisha follows Terry Denson to the bedroom; she seems so irritated and dissatisfied by what Terry had said to her.

"You know what? If you take sex as a priority in your life, we'll always be in fray in this house! I always come back home from work feeling so exhausted and weary; I don't have much time for sex and romance"

"Please put your duty behind this; I perceive nowadays you always try to trifle me. You have become so weird! It seems like you don't love me anymore."

"Who said that…..?"

"It's lucid that you remove your love from me"

"Don't reprimand me, Terry! Your problem is that you're trying to indulge yourself to me and I won't allow you to do such a thing! If am saying that I don't want to involve myself in sexual intercourse, I mean it and I won't….! Don't act like you're dictating me!"

"What is love Elisha?" He asks sadly

"Love? Mm mm… A great liking and affection"

"And sexual affection or passion"

"Yeah" Seem self-abash.

"Then elaborate this to me; do you think that your actions towards me resemble any kind of love whatsoever?"

"Precisely, love is not all about sex!"

"This is delusional Elisha! Without sex in marriage there is no love!"

"That is idle Terry! Don't be absurd! This is so drivel coming from your mouth Terry! Don't make me mad! We will have sex when the time is right! For now, I want to prepare for work! Wake up and stop acting like a bedridden person! Tsk!" She strides to the bathroom, her heart possessed by the ire.

Elisha is a beautiful medium woman with white sparkling eyes and brown skin, so attractive with her flat ass and amazing body shape, insight woman. She lives in a big house consisting of eight bedrooms with lounge, a kitchen and five bathrooms, a double garage as well as a swimming pool outside the house. She's stays with her husband and her seven-year-old daughter. She's a

26-year-old famous doctor. Her husband is a 30-year-old famous author, movies, and stories director; He's a short medium handsome man, shrewdness, and intellectual man.

Terry Denson gets out of the bed and go to check on his daughter Angel.

Angel is a smart intellect girl with brown skin like her mother, cunning eyes, and a beautiful face with sharp body shape.

He goes to her room and finds her awaken already; He greets her with a huge smile and goes to her and cuddle. He gives her a kiss on her forehead.

"You need to get out of bed and start preparing for school" he says this while still cuddling with her.

She emphatically gets off bed and goes straight to the bathroom.

Elisha enters Angel's room; she seems so yawn and ire.

"Don't ever exploit my feelings the way you did today! I hate to be spite by someone who always says he loves me"

"Don't be riot Elisha; Either I don't want mischief anymore!"

"You're the one who started this, Terry! You always try to break my heart! I'm having a lot of work problems on my mind!" She goes to the bathroom and snapping bath Angel and dresses her so quickly, kissing her all over the face.

"You look so beautiful my daughter." She says this with a huge smile on her face.

She embraces her and takes her for a ride to school with her jeep_trackhawk_V8.

"I hope you will be contemplating in doing something better in school rather than being tormenting other apprentices like you did before. Do you hear me? Don't be recalcitrant; be cooperative and polite at school."

They arrive at school; Angel seems so titillate when she sees her intimate apprentices waiting for her near her mother's car. She opens the door and runs towards them with a huge smile on her face and they embrace each other all three of them.

Elisha drives to work feeling so puzzling and tragic. She's worrying about the eccentric of her husband toward her when it comes to sex. She arrives to work and finds Eva busy treating the bedridden. Eva is Elisha's best friend; they used to gossip together and share some thoughts.

Terry is spending his day at home in inglorious confusing. Solicited himself-many questions that he never finds any answers, but all that comes to his mind is Elisha, accusing her that she may be in fornication with other man, hence he's trying to avoid it and contemplate of taking a bath and goes out for some fresh air.

"Yeah! Women!" He sighs and gets in his Mercedes_Benz_G63_V8 and drives to the coffee shop where he finds some old man sedentary on the table alone wearing a large jacket with black trousers and black shoes. His name is Thomas. Terry starred at him once and turned his attention to his phone while he waits for the coffee he had ordered.

"Hi! Young man! Come here!" Thomas

"What for old man? I'm feeling comfortable where I am!"

"Those rejuvenation folk of nowadays they are so possessed by recalcitrant toward older people!" Thomas

"What! What did you say old man?" Terry gets some temper.

He gets up from his chair and walks toward the old man trouncing him in his face.

"You need to have some sort of manners old man! We'll never feel pathetic for you because you are old man"

People inside Kalahari coffee shop are very shocked by the rabble-rouser that Terry is triggering at that coffee shop.

"Sir, you need to stop what you are doing before I kick you out!" The owner of the coffee shop says this arrogantly while staring Terry straight on his face.

"I hate mischief! But someone who takes us inferior really annoys me!" He sobs and scrambles out of the coffee shop. Thomas is a crippled old man. He kicked a stone when he was still young, and his big toe becomes damaged.

Terry Denson takes off from Kalahari coffee shop and rides to the club. On the way out he realizes that he must make a call to his best friend Simon! Simon is a tall man with a slender body. He's a rich young man who owns some of the big shops.

"Hey man! Are you busy?" Terry.

"Hey man! No, I'm not busy at all; I am just chilling with my cousin! Oh, is that you by the coffee shop? Simon seemingly confused.

"What?"

"Are you watching TV?"

"What's on TV?"

"Man! You're all over the news!"

"Ooh shirt! The media is trying to get in my nerves!"

"Man! You trounced an old man! What's going on with you?"

"I'm having a big problem! How about we meet at the gang club?"

"Cool I will be right there! Don't be chaos man! I'm coming to you, my man!"

# Chapter 2

Elisha is having a hectic day at the office. She is having a lot on her mind but deep down inside she knows what's really troubling her, having lack of libido towards her husband Terry Denson, but she has unconditional love for him.

"Eva! Do you think sex can be a priority in a relationship?"

"Oooh…. Yes! I think sex is an essential part in a relationship! I don't think man can approach us without intending to copulate." She gasps.

"In my opinion, I don't think sex is an important part of our lives! I was trying to cogitate why African countries get so impoverish, with that in mind, I realize that a lot of people are brainwashed in a way that it is like they have been poured the spirit of sexuality in their brain. That is why you may find that a lot of people are committed to copulating than maintaining their future. If you're habitual on sex, you'll find yourself disremembering about your future!"

"Ahhhhhh! This is so delusional, and it makes you immature! Sex is also a virtuous thing to our health!"

"But it's destroying our future! Lots of people focus on sex rather than many things!"

"Please mate, have sex! Sex is ecstasy of our body and affection of our emotional and relaxation of our inner spirit and give our body balance!" She blushes and then giggles.

"Don't tease me Eva" She giggles

"But just tell me! I don't get it, you're a married woman. How can you mosquitos' sex when you're married? Do you have a problem with Terry when it came to sex?"

"Eish, yeah! I'm having a huge problem!

"I sniff it!"

"I'm no longer interested in sexual intercourse with Terry."

"What!!" Seems so shocked "What are you trying to say?"

"I'm serious! I don't even feel him, but I still love him!"

"I don't get it! I think……. This is elaborated in my mind!  You said you love him; hence you don't feel him? How come?"

"He doesn't entertain me when we are having sex, even when he steps adjacent to me, I don't feel anything! It's melancholy me"

"Ooooh! My gosh! What is happening in this world people?" She becomes confused. "Then do you want to get rid of your marriage?"

 No!! Hell no! How can I………?"

"Then what is your plan….?"

"I'II just acts as if everything is okay on my relationship."
"What about Terry?"

"What do you mean?"

"You'll let him live like hell without having copulation with her wife? He will need to ejaculate as a man Elisha! She giggles.

"That is my problem! I can't make him zealous when am throb with pain in my pussy when i get copulating with him. It's so suffocating for me to sleep with Terry nowadays"

"I want to oblige you in that matter because Terry is a virtuous man. He doesn't deserve to be tormented."

"There is nothing you can do because this is inside my body! My whole body ejected the feeling for him."

"No! There are many ways that can help you bring back feelings for him! Does he make you wet when you're both preparing for copulation, or he just insert his penis into your vagina like you're getting raped?" She giggles.

"Ouch! Complicated! But maybe that is the matter, lack of romance when we have sex, because probable my man is not romantic in bed. I feel the pain when I'm having sex with him."

"Sometime in a prolonging relationship partners get wearisome to each other. But it's our duty as partners to make our relationship remain new each day of our lives."

"My relationship is in tiresome stage."

"Take your time and spend it with your man! Try to seduce him and try to always look tidy on his sight. Kiss him and hug him in the public when everybody is staring at you guys! Look at his eye and always say you really love him. You are supposed to tell him his weakness that he has when it comes to copulating. Don't let your man become misogynist; Go out for a date together and make him your best friend. You will see, your love will turn back to normal, and you will be thrilling again. Being in love is healthy my girl!"

Doctor Richie enters the hospital basement where Elisha and Eva were having their lunch.

"Elisha! I summon you to obliging me with a patient!"

"OK, Doctor Richie. I'm coming!"

**Chapter 3**


Terry arrives to the club; he seems heart broken and dizzy; eliciting to resolve problematic that he is facing with his wife Elisha. He lights the cigarette while he waits for Simon. He sees that Simon is taking prolong to arrive to the gang club; He decides to buy two vodka and two bottles of Hennessey. He's blowing smoke like nobody's business while staring at the people who are dancing inside the club. A Lot of people in that club ecstasy themselves by doing different things, some are making love with their partners romancing and deep kissing and dancing romantic dances. Terry looks at the door, he sees Simon entering the club; He becomes amused when he sees him.

"Hey! My man! How are you doing man?" Simon

"I'm trying man! I'm trying!" Terry

"So, what's really happening in your relationship?"

"She's cheating on me! She's fornicating with someone else!"

"Oh! No man! Elisha fornicating……? I don't think Elisha can put you in that dilemma man! Stop those illusion ideas! Elisha is deeply in love with you."

"Do you think I'm infatuated in my mind?"

"Yes! You are man! Stop being unreasonable! Find something that can lead you to get valid evidence than accusing her! Did you see her with another man?" He pours Hennessey to a glass and begins to drink.

"Actually, she doesn't want to have sex with me! Honestly am sniffing something going on with that woman!"

"Did you ask her why she's not interested in sex with you?"

"She told me that she comes home feeling exhausted! She's trying to be mendacious to me day and night!"

"Maybe this issue is instigating by your weakness in the bed!" He laughed.

"Don't start! Don't try to make me lunacy" he says this pointing his finger at Simon.

"But trying to figure it out, a lot of women trifling their man for sex when we don't make them wet firstly when we are preparing for sex. Try to ask her why she is trifling you for sex!"

"Stop contaminating my manhood! I'm good in bed!"

"Don't destroy your marriage by being senility in bed! Try to be conventional with your woman man!"

Terry seems to be getting drunk. He slightly removes his eyesight from Simon and start peeping at the beautiful woman who's dancing in front of him. She's so attractive, a beautiful woman with brown skin and sparkling eyes. She shows great tender smile to Terry.

The music is playing so well, and people seem so deeply in love with it, they're playing Lionel Richie's song 'Good Morning'

Terry looks so sensational by the way Monica is dancing. She is soliciting him to come adjacent to her and dance with her.

"Come and dance with me handsome! Come close to me!"

Terry feels so confused and ecstasy. He smiles and goes to her. He's doing some romantic dance with Monica while holding her waist and squeezing her body! They begin to develop some feelings to each other. Both seem self-abash while they are dance slow because disc jockey changed the song to 'Dance the Night Away' still Lionel Richie's song.

They both feel so passionate about each other. They start to kiss passionately, and they both feel so vitality. Terry breaths so heavily while Monica she's holding him tightly.

"Can we transit ourselves to another place?" Monica whispering in Terry's ears.

"Yes! Oh yes! I wish we can….! He's filled with feelings for Monica. His dick gets so harder that he can't control himself. Even Monica is so we.

"Let go!" Monica takes Terry's hand and emphatically try to run with him.

"Hold on! Let me say goodbye to my friend!"

"Okay! Be snappy please!"

"Hey buddy! I will be back shortly! Don't be terrified" He sniggers

"Wow! I thought now you perceive what brought a mischief on your relationship with Elisha."

"Please Simon! Let me distract my problem with that sexy girl."

"Stop being sneakily even you are having a problem with your wife man!"

"Man! Let me do this!"

"Do what?"

"Have Sex with her!"

"This is totally trespasses. Elisha is trying to tribute herself to you, but you want to mess up with her!"

"I know! But try to stay out of this!"

"Oh ok! I will! Let me stay out of this! But one day you will face inglorious pain man! Am serious! I'm crossing my fingers!"

Terry takes Monica by her hand and trek with her to hotel. They spend some zealous night yonder at hotel, were Terry thought Monica is so paramount at that night. He grips her waist and start to kiss her deeply, rubbing her whole body, throw her romantically to the bed and kisses her whole body, squeezing and rubbing her. Monica feels so wetter breathing heavily while she holds Terry on his ribs. They feel like they own the whole world on this night. They contact their eyes toward each other while Terry feels so titillating about this night. Terry inserts his penis on Monica's cookie and they both breaths so quick and heavily. Monica squeezing her hands slowly on Terry body kissing him likes nobody's business. She's fulfilling by Terry feeling that make her act like lunatic person.

Elisha is wondering about why her husband taking so prolong to arrive home. She checked her watch and finds that it's already twelve o'clock midnight. She picks up her phone and call him several times.

When Terry hears his phone ringing, he realizes it might be Elisha calling; He avoids it because he was so busy with Monica's cookie.

Elisha becomes so ire and frustrated. She's having a lot on her mind and that completely stops her from slumbering. She realizes that she must calls Simon.

"Hello!" Simon yearning

"Hello Simon!" Elisha

"Hey! Elisha." Yearning

"Sorry to disturb you so late!"

"It's okay! It's okay!"

"I wonder if you're with Terry, where you're now?"

"No! Terry just vanished at the club!"

"He Disappeared, to where?"

"I don't know!" Seems confused.

"Ohh! Okay! Thanks! Have a wonderful night!"

"Thanks, you too."

She hangs up her phone not knowing what to do because she's feeling so destructed. She shrieks while she's striding from her bedroom to Angel's bedroom! She throws herself on Angel's bed feeling so ire. She is cuddling Angel tightly while she's still crying and frustrated!

"Mommy" Angel

"Yes my child." Elisha

"Why are you here in my room? Did my daddy come back home?"

"No! My daughter! I just want to be with you!"

"Ok mommy! Can I ask you something?"

"Yes" She's uneasy about her husband

"Is everything going well between you and daddy?"

"Baby; It's the middle of the night now go to sleep please."

"Okay mommy!"

Elisha is not slumbering well cogitating about a lot of things about her husband.


**Chapter 4**


In the morning Elisha wakes up and prepare breakfast for her family as usual.

She hears someone knocking on the door outside. When she opens the door, she founds that it's Terry!

She looks at him holding her waist; She feels so weary when staring at him.

He enters inside the house looking so gawk! Elisha just looks at him gawping.

"Morning" Terry feels bashful

"Morning" Elisha possessed with anger

"I'm…!"

"Where have you been?"

"I was at… I slumbered at work!"

"Were?"

"I….."

"You slept at the club with girls? Huh?"

"No! That's not true! I slept at Simon's house!"

"What? Stop lying to me Terry! Stop…..!" She strikes him on his face.

"Are you slapping me Elisha?"

"Yes! What will you do?"

"You are such a bustard woman!"

"What?"

"Tsk!"

"Tell me! Precisely what do you want in your life Terry?"

"Nothing!" He says this and waddle straight to the bedroom.

"Do you think sex can give you a better future for your entire life? Huh?" She's wailing behind his back.

"Stop being vulgar Elisha!" He's swaying all over the bedroom.

Elisha denudes herself and throwing herself on the bed.

"Okay! Come! Come and having that sex that make you feel titillating!" She put her hands to her face and starts shrieking.

"Stop acting like a lunatic Elisha"

"I love you Terry, why are you torturing me like that?"

"You are the one who is torturing yourself by overthinking"

Terry waddles to the bathroom to take a bath and leave Elisha crying on the bed. He's acting like there is nothing happening between him and Monica as he's acting innocent to his wife Elisha! His phone rings on the bed and Elisha looks at it and find it that a lady called Monica is calling. She's trying to take it but she's shrinking to pick it up.

She is so eliciting herself about Monica who's appearing on the screen of her husband's cell phone.

"I don't get it. Who's Monica?"

Terry strides from bathroom to pick up his phone.

"Hello!"

"Hi! It's Monica!"

"Yeah Monica; How are you doing?"

"I'm doing fine and you?"
"I'm fine too!"

"Ohh! That's great! I still need you to adhere near me, my handsome!"

"Where can we meet?"

"At the gang club"

"What time?"

"I will call you."

Elisha staring at Terry seems inglorious and furious.

"Who's Monica?" Elisha.

"She is my client." Terry.

"Client meets at gang club?"

"Am going to fetch her at the club and trek together to my work." He said that obliquely.

"Is it a He or She?"

"She..." He's seeming bashful.

" Ohh! Ok!"

"She's Monica! Her name is Monica."

"Okay! I see!"

Terry dresses himself rapidly and takes a trek to the club to fetch Monica while Elisha stayed in bed, so confused and shedding tears.

"This love makes me feel like I'm diving deeper in the ocean." Elisha


**Chapter 5**


It's on a Sunday when Eva drives her BMW X5 to church. Eva is a white woman with a chubby body. She loves babbling and chatting with anybody she meets. When she's on the pavement of the road she meets Mrs. Chelsea walking to church.

"Hey! Mrs. Chelsea!"

"Hey! Eva. How are you?" She smiles.

"I'm fine Mrs. Chelsea." She giggles.

"That's so great!"

"Get inside the car we'll take this journey together!" She's looking so ecstasy.

"You're looking so beautiful young girl." She says this while she makes herself comfortable on the car sit.

"Ohh! Thanks Mrs. Chelsea."

They look so sensational to each other.

Chelsea is Elisha's mother. She's a slender insight woman with full of splendor life. She's a vitality woman with sparkling eyes and a pretty face.

"So! How is your friend doing?"

"You mean Elisha?"

"Yeah"

"Elisha is doing fine. But not entirely........" She said that showing self-abash.

"What do you mean not entirely?"

"I think we need to address this before something happen between Elisha and Terry. I thought the evil spirit is trying to interfere in Elisha and Terry's relationship."

"Please Eva! Please! Stop being oblique and say something!"

"Okay! Let me say it….."

"Say it!"

"Elisha told me that she's having lack of libidos when it comes to having copulation with Terry." She gasps and she's looking gawk.

"What?"

"Yeah, she just told me that…….!"

"Mm! Let try to be lucidity on this matter! Do you think Elisha fornicating with other man out there?"

"No! No! No Mrs. Chelsea! She can't do that!"

"How can she lose interest on copulating with her husband?"

"It just…."

"It's just what? Where do you think she get sex from? She's on fornication!"

"No! I think she's just tired of sex because Elisha is a hyperactive woman! Maybe she gets home exhausted."

"Lot of people get hyperactive, but there's something called feelings that attract two people to oblige in sex even when they feel exhausted."

"I know! But stop hypothesizing something that is not true about your daughter."

"You know? That girl is making me wander! Terry is virtuous man! Don't get worrying, I will solve her!"

They arrive to the church and Eva drives her car to the parking area. She's feeling self-abash after telling Mrs. Chelsea the issue of Elisha and her husband Terry. They get inside the church and start singing with the other members of the church.

# Chapter 6

Terry takes off to the gang club and finds Monica drinking Hennessey holding her cigarette by her left hand. He goes to her and embraces her, kissing her lips down to her neck, then he whispers in her ear.

"Let take a ride to hotel" Terry

"Wow really?" Monica

"Yes, my sexy woman."

"I thought your wife was going to be mad since you slumbered out yesterday."

"No! She didn't do that."

"Mm!                                        Okay!"
"Let's go"

He grabs her waist by his hand and takes a ride with her to hotel. They have a zealous journey on that trice, they're disputing about the fanciest car around the entire world and turn their topic to political paraphernalia.

They arrive to the hotel. Terry feels so abash because he perceived he strays of his conscience and he deliberately treacherous Elisha. He tries to dismiss all that his mind is thinking about Elisha and gets his focus back to Monica.

He pulls back the couch and make Monica sedentary sedate to the couch. He kisses her and pouring a tidbit of red wine on the glass and pass the glass of wine to her.

"Thank you my handsome!" She shows a shy face.

"It's my pleasure my pretty woman!" He smiles to her, and she smile back at him.

"You're so romantic Terry! I really want to always be adhering next to you. I don't want to lose you now. You rock my heart."

"You are the only girl I want to disburse my entire life with. I am not going to lose you or leave you. You rock my heart too."

She placed her lips to Terry lips and start kissing him slowly.

"You're exactly what my heart desire. You always remind me of a good time I once had in my past." She grips Terry by his T-shirt and pulls him closer to her.

"Terry!"

"Yes beautiful!"

"I want you to take all of me!"

"Yeah, but you must remember that I have a wife."

"I know, and I don't want to put myself in your marriage. I just want you, not your marriage."

"I'm yours! You're my dream girl."

"Why don't you allow me to give you something special?"

"What that something special?"

"Sex"

"Wow! I think I took prolong without soliciting about it. Let's make ourselves get tired." He smiles and seems so keen.

She grips his hand and run with him to the hotel room. People are just gawping at them while they run to the room.

Monica denudes herself faster seems so emotional, she puts her hands on Terry's shoulder and kisses him deeply and romancing his whole body. She seems to be getting so emotional and having uncontrollable feelings.

They finish fornicating and Monica puts her head on Terry's chest. Terry deeply feels in love with Monica.

"You are so prodigy in bed Terry." She smiles.

"Oh! Wow! I don't think so!" He sniggers.

"I was trying to probation your performance in bed! Mm! You are so prodigious!"

Terry feels so pressed but deep down inside his mind he is wondering why her wife Elisha trifles him when it comes to sex while Monica feels so great when she has sex with him. He thinks maybe Elisha has stopped loving him.

"Terry!" Monica.

"Yes!"

"Do you enjoying having sex with me?"

"Yeah, I always enjoy eating your cookie!" He laughs.

"Then, why don't you marry me officially?"

"What?" He becomes confused.

"I want you to marry me, Terry; then we could be together for the rest of our lives!"

"I have a wife, Monica!" He seems confused.

"Oh! Then why you enjoy inserting your penis in my cookie when you know that you have a wife?" She looks at him dingy.

"Please Monica! Let's stop this."

"Make me your second wife."

"How come?"

"Since you're already having sex with me!"

"Please Monica! Stop this!"

"You can't procrastinate what has already happen, It's already inevitable!"

"What…?"

"I'm pregnant." She shows her shy face.

Terry becomes uneasy and dizzy at that trice. He's frustrated and step down from the bed and rapidly dresses himself up quickly. He just disappears without saying a word to Monica.

"This is trespasses! Tsk! I will take my whole life to contrive to make that bustard pay." Monica said that while she dresses herself up. She takes her handbag and striding to the tar-road to wait for the taxi. Taxi hoots adjacent to her, she gets in and ride home.

# Chapter 7

Jennifer and Eva seem so fantastic at the hospital and having some witticisms about some colleague doctors. It seems so hard to Elisha to cooperate on her duty, she's just acting like she's fine, but it shows in her face that she's not fine.

"Elisha!" Jennifer

"Yeah" Elisha

"Why are you so sullen?" Jennifer

"Elisha! You need to stop acting like you're contrite to someone else here! You must dismiss something that doesn't give you peace inside you. We live once girly. There is no time for distress!" Eva

"Shrink from something that scorn you and be vitality. This is life that we are living now, it's a must to always feel happy buddy!" Jennifer

"Oh! Happy?" Elisha raised up her hands and shrilling. "I am fulfilled by hysterical!!!"

They all look at each other and laugh. Even though Elisha try to be hysteria, dismiss her thorny problems with her husband Terry at that moment but she's reticent on that matter because she was fulfilled by ire and savage.

They are having a good zealous conservation and a lot of fun.

It is raining heavily outside that a lot of things are floating on the water that is flowing on the ground surface.

Jennifer says goodbye to her colleagues Elisha and Eva. She takes a ride on her white Mercedes Benz G63_V8 back home feeling sensational by the zealous day that she spent with her colleague. She switches on her music and play a song by Lou Rawls called 'When love goes wrong'

She arrives at some gravel-road which has a huge pothole. Her front wheel lodge inside of pothole and there is no one near and passing by that road. She becomes confused and frustrated. She contemplates to call Richie. She picks up her phone and deal Richie's number.

"Hi! Doctor Richie!"

"Hello Jennifer."

"I am stuck in the gravel-road near your home at S.K street."

"Oh! Okay. I'm coming!"

"Okay! But try to hurry because it's already somber."

"Okay no problem."

Richie takes a fast jaunt with his car to oblige Jennifer. He arrives at that gravel-road were Jennifer is stuck.

"Hi! Jennifer!"

"Hi! I am stuck please oblige me……!"

Richie checks allover around Jennifer's car and peeps at her.

"Nothing we can do! You shall sleep at my place."

"Mm! I'm wondering what my man will be thinking about me yearning to come home! Let me call him first."

"Okay, call him."

She calls him several times, but his phone is turned off.

"Voicemail"

"Let go to my place."

They take off to Richie's place. Richie he's a tall white doctor who stays in town. He's paternal with three children, two daughters and one son. He spends most of his time playing with his children when he's at home. His wife is a teacher at Progress secondary school. She's a tall woman who has a warm, kind, and loving heart.

They arrive at Richie's home. Jennifer gets some outrageous entering the house; She pretends to smile but deep down inside she perceives that Richie's wife Gloria may be acting eccentrically to her.

She's having no choice rather than to enter Richie's house. She enters the house and finds Gloria sedentary on the couch watching TV.

They both peep at each other.

"How are you, Jennifer?" Gloria

"I'm fine!" She smiles.

Jennifer does not perceive that Gloria known her name. She becomes outrageous when she heard Gloria calls her by name.

"Oh! Do you know my name?"

"Yes! Richie always talks about his colleagues."
"Oh! Richie?"
Richie is playing passionately with his children on the ground near the couch.
"He always said that he works with lunatic people with plenty of hysteria, that why sometimes he takes yearning to come back home because he loves to laugh."
"Yah I know."
"He said you are the one of lunatic people."
"Oh!" They both laugh widely.
"Come! Come and oblige me with something in the kitchen."
They get a sensational night together full of fun and witticisms. Jennifer spends her night at Richie's

house. She's emphatically trying a lot to call her husband several times, but his phone is off.

Thomas is also wondering a lot about his wife Jennifer who is not coming home; it's already twelve o'clock midnight. He drives to the hospital to look for her but couldn't find her. He becomes tragic and tormenting.

He is swaying all over his bedroom fulfilled by ire. The problem on his phone was network but Thomas doesn't notice his phone's network because his phone was not having a proper network.

In the morning Richie goes to the room where Jennifer was sleeping, he wakes her up.

"Jennifer! Wake up; I got someone who can help you get your car out of the pothole."

"Okay." She's yawning.

"We need to be quick!"

She gets up and dresses herself and quickly gets out.

"Let's go!"

They hurry to the gravel-rod where Jennifer's car got stuck. She finds her car has already been taken out of the pothole.

"Hey man!"

"Hey! I'm already done with my work!"

"Thanks man! She was so desperate!"

"Thank you very much" Jennifer feels grateful towards Richie, and she takes out some money and disbursing Jimmy.

"Thanks madam!" Jimmy.

"Richie let me rush to my man at home. He may be missing me already!"

They all get stimulated and laugh widely.

"Goodbye man!" Jennifer.

"Goodbye Jennifer!" Richie.

Jennifer carries on with her journey home. When she gets there, she finds her husband Thomas swaying at the seating room.

"Morning my hubby"

"Where have you been?"

"I got some…….!"

"Shut up!"

"Oh! I didn't perceive thing will get pessimist!"

"Oh! Don't even say a word, do you hear me?" He takes out a gun and points it on her forehead.

"Then, are you trying to outrageous your wife by your gun?"

"Kneel down!"

"What? Oh! Hold on! What are you doing Thomas? What has gotten on to your mind?"

"I said kneel down and don't say a word!"

"You're terrifying me, Thomas!" She gets shocked and she's sobbing inglorious while also being possessed by frustration.

"I said shut up!!"

He pointed his gun on Jennifer chest and sigh.

"Jennifer! I love you so much, but you treat me like trash. You decide to cheat on me and treacherous behind my back. He sobbed to cry.

"I was…..! I was…….!" She's so confused, and her heart is filled with terror.

He pulls the trigger of his slug gun and shoot Jennifer on her chest.

She falls and lay on a pool on her blood.

He shoots another bullet on her back and he run away. People who heard that rowdy of gun goes there to see what has happened. They find Jennifer laying down on her blood. They urgently call the police.

Thomas rides to the river holding a rope and he hangs himself on the big tree near the river.

**Chapter 8**

It is nine o'clock in the morning when Elisha arriving at her mother's home. She gets so vivacious when she finds her mother washing dishes, she laughs wildly when she points at her mother with her right hand.

"Oh! What in the world?" Elisha laughs.

"Oh! My daughter"

She points at her mother with her finger while she giggles.

"It's been so long without seeing you cook and wash the dishes."

"I'm a woman, remember!"

They both laugh.

"Where's your helper?"

"I gave her some break to go home so that she may see her family."

"Okay! Then cook!" She laughs widely.

She goes to the sitting room and make herself comfy on the sofa.

"My daughter"

"Yes mom!" Elisha says that showing a great enthusiasm.

"I called you because my head was throbbing with pain caused by you and your husband Terry!"

"Oh! Mom"

"I tried to make you thrive from when you were still young my daughter."

"I know mom"

"Why are you giving your husband a tough time my daughter?"

"I don't get you mom! I'm confused. What are you talking about?"

"Don't fool me, Elisha! You know exactly what am talking about!"

"I don't mom…!"

"Eva told me about all the issues between you and your husband. She told me that you're procrastinating your husband in bed."

"Oh! I don't have a word for that." She seems timid.

"My daughter, we need to make this conversation social! You're a grown woman! Let talk women to women!"

"This will be a thorny conversation to me mom. Talking to you about sex? Mom, be realistic!"

"Please just take me as your best friend for today!"

"Okay! Then what the matter?"

"The matter is you don't spend much time with your man, I'm talking sexually."

"Mom, you know that I'm always busy!"

"My daughter!"

"Mom"

"Look outside all over the world. Everybody's hyperactive because there is no time to relax in this world. You need to sort out your mind and manage your time to do everything that requires your attention."

"I know!"

"You need to balance your working time and the time you spend with your husband. Do you know what is destroying a lot of people?"

"No! What it is?"

"Pride"

"Mom"

"A lot of successful women find it difficult to be in a prosperous relationship because of pride. Pride kills."

"Oh!"

"You need to balance your life because even a relationship is a basic future of our lives. Don't stray even one of your single futures. If you fail one of your futures, you fail your entire life. Do you want to fail your life?"

"No mom" She seems shy.

"Then you need to give much time to your husband. You need to have a moral sex with your husband."

"Mom please"

"Sex is the one paraphernalia for building the strongest bond in a relationship. You need to always have sex with your husband to make you relationship last."

"I thought I had lost feeling for Terry, that's why I don't enjoy having sex with him."

"That happens in a lot of relationships. Frays in a relationship causes a lack of interest in sex between partners."

"Then what can I do to regain my feelings for Terry?"

"You need to stop fighting and spent most of your time in a zealous relationship. Fighting is a best foe to destroy interest in sex with your partner."

"I will try mom. Let drop this topic."

"Spend more time with your husband to avoid losing him to other girls. Be her best friend and don't become dread to always copulate with him. Try to rehabilitate your marriage"

"Okay thanks mom."

She goes back to the kitchen to finish dishing her plates and cooking. She makes dessert for Elisha and gives it to her.

"Thanks mom you're a life saver."

Mrs. Chelsea smiles and goes back to the kitchen.

Elisha is busy watching news on TV while she nourishes herself with dessert.

"What? What the hell?" Elisha seems frustrated.

"What's happening?" Mrs. Chelsea

"Maybe I'm having a nightmare!"

"I said what is happening."

"Jennifer got shoot by her husband mom" she says that sobbing. "He killed her! He killed my best friend!" She throws the plate down and brake into tears.

"What the hell?" Mrs. Chelsea

Elisha is crying like a baby without the ability to control herself.

"He killed her mom! Men are such horrible monsters!"

"That's so terrible!!" She looks sadly at Elisha and puts her in her arms.

"Mom" She's having plenty of tears in her eyes.

"My daughter." With her still in her arms.

"What going on with men of nowadays?"

"It's okay my child, it okay!"

"It's not okay mother! And it will never be okay! We are so sick and tired of those monsters' called men who express the repulsive fatal in women. We are tired mom! We are worried as women!" She sobbed.

"Try to be strong my child. It will all be sorted." They both hug each other tightly.

**Chapter 9**

Terry and Simon go to Terry's studio. Terry's sullen thinking about Monica's pregnancy and how Elisha will react when she finds out. He is trying to tell Simon about the matter; however, it seems so difficult for him to say a word to his friend Simon. Simon seems cordial chilling on the car seat. He's jabber and making a lot of jokes that makes him laugh wildly, Terry feels so monotonous and reluctant by Simon's witticism.

"Man, please! Just……….!"

"What?"

"Just keep quiet! I'm having a lot on my mind."

"What going on?"

"Man! I'm impregnated Monica."

"What? Tell me that you're joking!"

"No man, I'm not! I'm frustrated; I don't know what to do!"

"Man! You dive your head in deep cold water! How can you do that man?"

"Don't judge me man! I make mistakes just like everybody does!"

"No! You're mendacious! This is no mistake, you did it deliberately!"

"Don't judge me! I'm flounder and it's ponderous to me to conquer this situation!"

"I'm not judging you! I counsel you that day, hence you proceed with your diligence."

"Help me man! What if she finds out?"

"I think she will kill you!"

"I got so fallen in fond with Monica! I tried to stray away from her but it's so dodgy for me to stray out of her. She takes all of me, my heart and my mind also."

"Now, you regret coming because you did it with full of impulsive. But you impudent Elisha shame, she doesn't deserve this."

"She's the one who made me do that; she makes me suffocate with depression since she keeps on denying me sex."

"You're sneaky Terry. You don't want to man up!"

"You're 29 years old now! You're not even in a courtship but you're just wailing on me like a baby. Find a woman and get married!"

"Ah! That's idles! Then what's you're contrive?"

"I want to build her a house so that she can live with my child."

"What about Elisha?"

"Elisha is my wife, and she will be lucidity on that."

"O! Okay!"

"I always tell you not to stick your nose in my business!"

They finally get to Terry's studios. Terry starts to compile his stuff orderly but his face expresses that he's not blissful at all.

Monica's swaying all over paddock near her cottage cogitating a lot about her pregnancy and trying to think of ways to rehabilitate her relationship with Terry.

She picks up her phone and she elect to send outrageous message to Elisha.

Elisha has already gotten home; she receives a creepier massage. She ponders while try to perceive the person who's sending her such a message, the message stated the following:

'Elisha! You must eliminate yourself from my man before something sinister happen to you'

Elisha becomes so outrageous, she immediately forwards that message to her husband Terry; But she realizes that he's cheating on her with other girls, she becomes feeble and fearsome.

Terry becomes muddled after seeing that message from Elisha.

"I want to go now!" Terry

"To where?" Simon

"We have some problem that I must quickly figure out"

"What's happening man? Talk to me!"

"I think Monica sent a shocking message to Elisha!"

"What? What the hell!!"

"Let me go fix this mess."

"This will turn out to be ponderous to your marriage."

"Shut up!"

He walks to his car and drives to Monica's house. Monica is bob at paddock pondering what she may do to save her relationship with Terry. She peeps at the road which is heading to her home and sees Terry's car advance faster to her home. She peeps to the horse paddock and smile. Terry steps out of his car seeming so worried and he is striding to where Monica is standing.

"What're you trying to do Monica? Do you want to destroy my marriage?"

She sighs.

"Ah! Tell me …….."

"Tell you what Monica?"

"The first day we meet, we were deeply sentimental and show commitment in having sex."

"And then?"

"Now since I am carrying your child in my womb you just treat me like trash; Why Terry?"

"It's not like that, Monica; all that I want to do is to deal with this issue in a conventional way!"

"What conventional way Terry? This is absurd. You 're doing things in an unconventional way!"

"I'm trying to fix our issues Monica! Please give me some peace of mind!"

"You were titillating inserting your penis in my cookie Terry! You slept with me! I'm not your horse that you may ride on it and do whatever you what to do on it!"

"Oh!"

"I'm a human being! You can't just sleep with me and throw me away like a waste product!"

"What do you want me to do because I have already told you that I have a wife!"

"You need to marry me!"

"We were just fornicating Monica!"

"What Terry? Do you think we were having sex for nothing?"

"Let me pay you a price for that..!"

"I'm not a prostitute Terry! I love all that other women love; there is no woman who doesn't want to be in a marriage in this entire world. I was having a big dream about my future life; I told myself that I want to have a happy family with someone who's famous in this country; and I found you Terry, you made my dreams come true. You made my heartbeat smoothly." She kneels in front of Terry. "Don't abandon me, Terry; Am deeply in love with you." She says this while shedding tears.

Terry seems so confused. He picks Monica up and embraces her. His face expresses penitence for trespass on Elisha.

"Stop crying baby! Stop crying!"

She wipes off her tears while she holds Terry tightly.

"I love you, Terry!"

"It's okay babe! It's okay."

## Chapter 10

Elisha is busy watching TV, Terry arrives back home seeming bashful when he sees Elisha peeping at him.

He greets Elisha and waddle straight to bedroom.

"Wait! Where are you going?" Elisha

"I'm going to take a shower." Terry

"Don't take me like a lunatic person Terry! Are you cheating on me?" She seems so sad

"No Elisha! I can't do that to you!"

"You want to act innocent when deep down inside your heart you know you are mendacious! Huh? Are you trying to fool me? You always boob to me and act like everything is okay Terry!"

"Elisha! We need to stop fighting and solve things in conventional way!"

"Terry! Your girlfriend sent me a message on my phone! To your wife's phone! Then you say we must do things in a conventional way? Huh?" She picks the plate and throws it to his head, and she rashly snaps toward him, and she smack him on his face.

He starts bleeding on his head and nose.

"You hurt me, Elisha!"

"You deserve it! You compel our marriage to become infatuated! You scorn me! You're impulsively to destroy all that my heart is holding for this relationship!"

"Stop being imprudence! I love you Elisha and am sorry for my trespass which I did to you. You don't deserve this!" He starts crying. "You don't deserve to be scorn! I made a very huge mistake and I'm sorry, I contrite for my wrongdoing towards you!" Elisha covers her face and cry.

"But you spite me deliberately Terry! You don't love me anymore!"

He hugs her cordially and puts his palm to Elisha neck.

"Elisha! You're the only girl that I put my love and my trust on."

He adjacent his lips to Elisha lips and deeply kiss her. Elisha withdraws her body from Terry and takes some white towel and erasing Terry blood which sheds from his head and nose.

"I think you're no longer reluctant now?" Terry

"I'm sorry Terry." Elisha

"Let's make a truce for the sake of our marriage to exceed more and more my love."

"Sure! No fight anymore!" She smiles

"You such a beautiful woman I have ever meet; You're so valuable and paramount to my life! The beauty of your face makes me always remember the day I met you. Your devotion arose my compulsion feeling to always adhere to you, you such a nice woman!"

"Oh! I was really missing those devotional words coming from your mouth!" She moves close to Terry and look him in his eyes. "I'm having that compulsion that compels me to always love you more and more! You always make me mad when you act strange toward me because I can't dispose from this love for us; you're so momentous to my life."

"I will never deprive on you my sweetheart, I promise!"

Elisha embraces Terry and murmur to his ear!

"I miss to be together in one bed."

"What?" He mumbles. "You mean we shall…!"

"Yes"

"Okay!" He picks her up by his arms and tread with her to bedroom; he put her on the bed and passionately kiss her, rubbing her boobs and slowly squeezing her ribs. He strips her clothes kissing her allover her body, she becomes wet and takes Terry's clothes off.

They start having copulation. Terry seemingly pondering a lot about his reticent and it deplore him because he doesn't find a way to acknowledge Elisha about the issue of impregnating Monica.

Elisha feels pain when they are busy copulating, but she didn't say anything rather she tolerates the pain and wait for Terry to ejaculate. She peeps at his face and finds out that Terry is not enjoying her, his mind seemed to be somewhere. She becomes edge and ejecting Terry from her body.

"What now?" Terry

"What are you thinking about when you're with me?"

"I am not thinking about anyone, am serious!"

"Stop fooling me! You are thinking about the girl you fornicated with her yonder!" She yelps while covering herself with blanket.

"But we made an oath that we'll never fight again?"

"Whatever! I'm really sick and tired by monotonous that usually happen between us!" She braces on the floor and dresses herself. "This relationship is become famished!"

"What have I done?" He asks sadly and yelling.

"Tsk! Maybe you need probation of being in marriage rather than wasting my time."

She treads to her car and rides to her companion Eva.

Terry is being left at the house trying to make himself valiant. He's waddling up and down on the bedroom seeming vertigo.

Elisha finds Eva at the tar-road waiting for her to take a ride to a vacation.

Eva saw Elisha stepping out of her car and she feels vivacious inside; she smiles to her and goes to hug her.

"How are you doing my chum?" Eva

"I'm not okay Eva." Elisha

"Oh! I know!"

"Eish"

"This dilemma between you and Terry is becoming monotonous!"

"Let's go to a park! I don't want to talk about this anymore!"

They take a ride to the park instead since they couldn't find an empty parking spot. They arrive at the park and sit on the bower then they start to drink syrup.

The park consists of two big swimming pools and several swings and variety of trees

Monica sees Eva and Elisha while she's busy swimming. She gets out of the pool and swift to them and greets them.

"Hi guys!" Monica greets Eva and Elisha while she's smiling

"Hi" Elisha and Eva seem to smile back at Monica.

"You feasibly seem so familiar to me."

"Who's?" Eva seems confused

"You; which school did you attend?"

"You mean secondary or….?"

"Primary"

"Johnson's primary school"

"Oh! You're…..?"

"Eva"

"Monica"

"Oh! Monica! Monica! Moo….!" She's seeming meditating about Monica's name "Oh! Are you that mad girl that I attended with at grade 7?" She becomes stimulated by remembering Monica.

"Wow! Yes, I am!"

Ohh! It has been a long time!"

"Yah! How are you doing?"

"I'm doing fine"

"Okay! Oh! May I join you and spend this zealous time with you guys?"

"Oh! No problem; Join us." Elisha

"I don't think we know each other." Monica said that while she looks at Elisha's face.

"Yah! My name is Elisha!" She greets with a handshake.

"I'm Monica!" She smiles.

Monica is trying to pretend while she deeply knows Elisha for a long time. She knows that Elisha is Terry's wife.

"Wow! You're pregnant?" Eva

Monica smiles.

"Yes, I am!" Monica

"Congratulation, you're going to be a mother!" She says this while she's shrilling.

"Yah! I am a mother to be, but you can't be so excited."

Ohh! Why baby?"

"I just got snag since my man has been acting eccentrically towards me; He left me!"

"Oh! Shirt! Why, men are so rubbish?" Eva

"Men don't have a tactful; they are clumsy when it comes to treating their woman." Elisha.

"I thought I was the only one who's facing this dilemma." Monica

"No! I'm having a huge problem in my marriage, and it scorns me day and night." Elisha

"Oh! What's happening my chum?" Monica

"My man probably cheating on me."

"O! That issue of cheating, mm! I'd rather quit my marriage if my man does that to me!" Monica

"Quit? You need to try to be philosophical no matter how hard it is on your relationships!" Eva

Mrs. Vanessa is standing adjacent to were Elisha, Eva and Monica are sedentary.

Mrs. Vanessa is 68 old women with a slender body shape; she has a brown skin with spackling eyes. Her husband died on a car accident. Now she's living with her 39 years old son. She enjoys spending most of her time with young woman and sometimes with youth. She's a bilingual woman.

"That's some wonderful words coming from you, my daughter!" Mrs. Vanessa.

"Thank you!" Eva

"My name is Vanessa. Hej! Vad gör ni ute i stormen?"

"We are just having a dispute as woman."

"Okay, fine. But when I consider your topic girls; you're totally deluding each other!"

"How?" Monica seems tedious.

"When I was a woman like you; my husband used to Couse anxious on our marriage, but residual which I leant is that; you must always avoid having a reticence towards your relationships, communication in your relationship is the best way to deal with your men. You need to be optimistic in each challenge you're facing in your marriage." Vanessa.

"If someone cheats in a relationship you must retaliating him/ her with cheating too!" Monica

"That's not an appropriate way to live. Never indulge yourself to be a laughingstock by the men. Men can play you like a basketball and leave you like a trash." Vanessa

"But Elisha's man shows that she's redundant towards him." Monica

"Love is complex." Vanessa

"What do you mean?"

"Sometimes you will find yourself in an irritable environment which makes you feel like you have to be distant from your man, but it doesn't mean you don't love him anymore; you need to give yourself time to resurrect the love you got the first time you meet with him."

"Elisha! You need to abdicate to that kind of love before something abominate happen to you, because men of nowadays are so horrible."

"We know, but she must firstly be tolerant and fore-sight for her marriage because she may lose the virtuous man by the little mistakes which he had done."

"Ah! He has already showed her that he's a dog!" Monica

Elisha and Eva peeps to each other and laugh.

"Elisha my daughter, don't listen to these persecute drivel words from your friend, just try to be philosophical for the survival of your marriage. Be shrewd and love your man until you find out what is really going on with him."

"This is abhorred; you need to dispose yourself from us because we don't need to hear the issue of man killing woman in our country!"

"Okay! But Elisha! I hope you shall have amorous with your man."

"Okay have a good journey to your home! Thank you so much for your wonderful advice!" Elisha raises her hand and say goodbye.

"We need to go too." Eva said that while she's looking at Elisha

"Okay! It also getting dull!" Elisha

"We'll see you when we meet again Monica!" Eva

"Sure chums!"

Elisha and Eva walks to their car while they're traveling abreast.

"Did you hear that she was trying to make you lose abide to your man? Yo! Girl with jealousy!"

"Oh! Don't take it serious, maybe she's trying to defend me."

"Defend you on what?"

"On Terry. Maybe she's sniffing something horrible."

"Oh okay!"

Monica was just standing on ground dingy at Elisha. Elisha and Eva steps in their cars and drive to their homes.

Elisha's feeling contrite after Vanessa said those words, she feels like she did trespass to her husband Terry.

She arrives home and find Terry lying on the bed looking like he's bilious, she greets him seems bashful.

"Hi" Elisha greet Terry seems bashful

Terry sprang by his feet on the floor acting like he's sprightly.

"Hi, my love, I was so worried about you!"

"Oh okay!"

"Where have you been?"

"Please my husband let's stop acting like we're okay when we're not…!"

"Okay!" He seems like there is something making him inglorious.

Elisha waddles near her husband and sits next to him on the bed. She looks Terry in his eyes.

"Terry, I tend to have a problem when we're having sex."

"What do you mean? O! You mean I'm not good in bed?"

"No! It's not like that, I….! I want to say….!"

"You want to say what?"

"I'm no longer having feelings for you when we are having copulation, but I don't mean I no longer love you."

"Are you sleeping with someone else out there?"

"No! Let's stop accusing each other and imploring on solving our issue."

"Okay! What make you stray your feelings from me?"

"Maybe you're inadequate in romance that makes me to not become wet and cum when we're copulating. Don't be impetuous because we are trying to solve our problem."

"Okay, I'm so happy that you are becoming open to me! Ok, how can we solve this…..?"

"O! Thanks! I thought you were going to talk slandering toward me?"

"I may… but I'm trying to save you and my relationship, and I thought communication is the best way to save any relationship."

"Oh okay.

Terry's phone rings, when he picks it up he finds it is an unknown number appearing on his phone screen.

"Who's calling? Elisha.

"I don't know, let me take this."

He takes two steps and then answer the phone.

"Hello!" Terry

"Hello!" Carol

"I'm Carol, friend of Monica…!"

"Okay what do you want?"

"Monica's at the hospital now, she's about to give birth!"

"What?"

"You must come to care Centre hospital immediately!"

"Okay I'II be there as soon as possible!"

"Okay!"

Terry peeps at Elisha. His facial expression shows that there is something that he's trying to hide from Elisha.

"Who was calling?" Elisha

"It's someone who solicited me to oblige him with something?"

"Is it Simon or some of your colleagues?"

"Some of my colleagues"

"Oh, but why are you looking quail"

"Nothing, It's nothing"

"Terry! I'm you're women! Don't be shy, you can talk to me about anything that may be bothering you because we need to be coherent and be helpful to each other as a couple!"

"Okay my love!" He shows a great simper kisses her on the forehead. "I shall be with you shortly!" He smiles, takes one of his jacket and rides to care Centre hospital"

Monica's trying to push harder for her unborn child to be born! She's sweating all over her body.

"You need to push harder; the baby is coming; Push!" Nurse

Monica's clamor showing that she's in huge pain.

The nurses try harder to help Monica give birth in an appropriate way; finally, Monica is congenital to a male baby that looks like his father Terry. She is laying at the hospital bed feeling dizzy.

Terry arrives at hospital and find Carol sitting on a chair.

"Hi, I hope you're Carol?" Terry

"Yes! I am!" Carol

"Where's Monica?"

"She's in the maternity ward; she has already given birth to a baby boy." She smiles

"Wow! How do you know that?"

"I heard them ululating saying that Monica has given birth to a beautiful boy."

"Oh my gosh! Thanks."

"Can we enter inside?"

"Not now, they must first summon us; let us try to be patient until they call us to come inside."

"I can't be patient for prolong. I want to see my child and the mother of my child."

"Hi Carol! Nurse

"Yes!" Carol

"You can come inside, she's awake!"

"Okay! I'm coming."

"Can I……!" Terry

"Who're you…..? Are you…!" Nurse

"Terry! The father of the child…!"

"I know you! You're a celebrity"

"Ahh! Let's forget about that! May I enter inside so that I may see my child?"

"Yes, come in!"

They enter inside the maternity ward. Terry's carrying food and some fruits with a plastic bag.

He sees Monica holding the baby, he immediately strides towards her and hold her hand and kisses her on her forehead.

"How're you feeling my love?"

"I'm feeling so dizzy!"

"You are going to be okay! Just try to be tolerant for this short moment!"

She looks at Terry's face and smiles.

"I love you Terry"

"It's okay!"

"He looks like you!" She smiles

"He's, my boy! He must resemble his father." He smiles too.

"Time is up for the visitors; she needs some time to res." Nurse

"When can you discharge her?"

"Tomorrow"

"Okay"

Terry smiles at Monica.

"I'II be back tomorrow in the morning to fetch you."

"Okay my darling! Let me get some rest!"

Terry goes back home with Carol. There is no conversation between the two along the way because Terry's cogitating about buying a house for Monica. He immediately picks up his phone and call Joseph.

Josephs in the real estate business. Terry dials Josephs number and call him.

"Hi man what's up?"

"Cool man!"

"I want us to meet very fast, I need something!"

"What is it?"

"I want to buy my girlfriend a house man."

"Good for her, she's a lucky girl". He loughs.

What do you mean?"

"I'm having a house in the suburb which consists of four-bedroom, kitchen, and study room, three bathroom and lounge, also a swimming pool outside, I think it will be perfect."

"Okay how much?"

"It will cost you more than 3 million dollars!"

"3 million dollar and above or only 3 million dollars"

"Only 3 million dollars"

"Okay let me drop someone and after that I'II come see you man! I indeed want to buy that house for my girlfriend man!" Terry shows that he's eager to buy that house.

"You're so loving man! spoil your women man!"

"Thanks man"

Terry drops Carol at her gate and drives back to Joseph. He finds Joseph at the pub, and they greet each other, Joseph takes Terry to the owner of the house. They ride to the municipality to sign an agreement of selling the house to Terry (change of ownership) then Terry pays for the house cash, and they give him the keys of the house. He's eager for Monica to move in since the deal is sealed.


## Chapter 11

He drives to his home, and he finds Elisha cooking while wearing some sexy outfit. He gets adjacent to her and holds her at her back.

"Something smells good!"

"Oh; Really?"

"Taste some."

He tastes the food.

"Mm; wow! It's testes so delicious! It makes me so ravenous."

"That's how your women feels when she's near you, I'm feeling so relish!"

"Wow! That's why I'm feeling so fond and devoted which always pours from my heart and flows within my veins and makes my heart adhesive with your adorable heart."

She hugs Terry and kisses him on his lips

"You're my hunk man that I never want to lose!"

"Oh! Finish your cooking and nourishes us with your pleasant food."

"Ag! I thought maybe you will help me cook."

"No! I want to watch the game between Man united and Man city! It's a derby remember?"

"Oho! I forgot about that! Please come and finish cooking; I have a great desire to watching this match."

"Oh! No! Finish what you have already started." He laughs.

"You are going to starve all night; I'II finish cooking in the middle of the night!"

"Whatever!" He laughs.

Terry goes to the lounge room and turns the TV on and watches the derby. He isn't concentrating on the derby as he's thinking about his son and Monica. Elisha comes to where her husband is sitting and sits next to him; she puts her head on Terry thighs. She's scratching the beards on Terry's chin with her finger.

"We're so scintillating when we try to avoid being belligerent to each other my love, I wish that it will always be like this in any day of our life!" Elisha

"Don't worry my love! You will always be the woman in my life." Terry.

Elisha immediately peeps at the TV and seem confused

"Why this couch always benching Rashford and Jesse Lingard?" Elisha

"And even this one of Man city he benches Zinchenko and Foden!" Terry

"Foden got injured in the last match when they played against Liverpool."

"That's my team! Liverpool is my team! Unlike your Manchester united, they always get beaten by the small teams!"

"We're settling on number three on the league table man!" She smiles

"My Liverpool is in number two!" He laughs.

"Whatever!"

They both have a great night dispute a lot about soccer.

In the morning Terry wakes up and prepare for his journey to the hospital. But he initially goes to the furniture shop to buy furniture for the new house that he bought for Monica and his son. He spends more than 100 000 dollars in buying that furniture. He did all those things behind Elisha's back. He makes sure all those furniture that he bought for Monica new house is slotted in appropriate way in the house.

He drives faster to hospital and finds out that Monica's already discharged. He helps her by opening the door for her to enter inside the car.

Monica seems very excited regarding Terry's actions towards her from the day she gave birth to his son.

"I named him bonafide." Monica

"Oh! That's a nice name! Why did you name him that?" Terry

"Because….!" She smiles.

"Because what?"

"Because he proceeding the genuine of my life which I meant to be in my past time sincerely!"

"What do you mean?"

"Like I said before, I always used to tell myself that I want to fall in love with a celebrity!"

"Oh! Okay!"

"Yah! Then why are you turning to the right? Have you forgotten where I live?"

"No, I haven't?"

"Then where are you taking us?"

"We're just riding to spend some time together."

"Terry this is not a good time for traveling."

"I know."

Oh! Okay." She seems disordered by Terry action.

Terry' drives while he's sullen. He enters the house he bought for Monica without saying anything to her.

"Are you crazy?" Monica

"Why?" Terry

"Be coherent and shrewd Terry!!" She yells at him.

"Coherent and shrewd on what"

"Terry please, you need to try to be rational. We can't visit people while I'm in this situation! Our child is eligible to be seen by other people for now!"

"Get out of the car and step down!"

I'm not getting out of the car with this child"

"I said get out of the car Monica." He yells at her.

"Ooh! Ok!" She becomes outrageous and muddled.

"Out" Terry yells at Monica again

She immediately gets out of the car seemingly shocked however trying to act bravely towards Terry whereas she's scandalized by Terry action.

"What the hell is that?" Monica

"Come here" Terry

They walk towards the door of the house. Terry knocks on the door and laugh. He takes out the keys in his pocket and tries to unlock the door but he acts like it's awkward for him to unlock the door.

"Just try, it's awkward for me to unlock it." He smiles

"I can't just unlock somebody else's house" Monica

"Just unlock it!" He yells.

Monica becomes strange by the way Terry's yelling at her.

"Okay! Let me try."

He hands her the keys, and she unlocks the door.

"Who's the owner of this house?" Monica

"Get inside!" Terry

"You can't drag me inside the house of a stranger Terry!"

"I said get inside the house!"

"You don't even want to listen to me, what's going on!"

"I don't care! I said get inside!"

"Okay! Then,….." She gets inside and puts the baby down on the sofa.

"You were saying?" Terry

"Who's the owner of this house because…..?" Monica

"It's you."

"What?"

"This house belongs to you." Terry

"Don't fool me Terry don't try to rejuvenate me I'm not a child anymore!"

"Oh! Rejuvenate girl! Do you see other people in or outside the house except us?"

"No!"

"Then why're you getting confused? This house and everything in it house belong to you and our son!"

Monica becomes stands like a statue and tears begin to run down on her face.

"Terry! Why are you doing this to me?"

"Because you're the mother of my child"

She cries and goes to him and hug him.

"You're a very special man; this house is so ravishing." She says this while still sobbing due to titillation of what Terry just did for her.

"It's just as beautiful as you!" Terry

"Terry! You're wonderful and benefactor of my life!"

"Okay! Let me go home!"

"No! You're not going anywhere today! I want to be with you all night in this new house with our baby! Give me a tour of the house before bonafide wakes up."

"Okay let start outside!"

They go outside of the house holding each other. Monica's feeling so zealous and sensational because of what Terry did for her; she's just shrieking all over the house because she's having uncontrollable happiness deep down her heart.

"Love is good for our health!" Monica says this while she's looking Terry straight on his face.

## Chapter 12

Elisha's at home keeping herself busy by irrigating the flowers in the garden; she's thinking about her lovely night with her husband Terry. She realizes that it is getting dark and rapidly get inside the house to compel Angel to take a bath.

"Mommy; why does dad come home late nowadays?"

"He shall be on his way back home now, just focus on taking a bath!"

"I'm having a problem with my dad's attitude mom!"

"What do you mean?" She asks muddling.

"He doesn't spend time with me like he used to!"

"Finish bathing and stop acting like a child; you're no longer a child!"

"Okay mom!"

Elisha says this and walks to the sitting room to watch soccer highlights. She realizes that she must make a call to her husband because it's almost half past eight hence Terry is not coming back home. Terry is not taking her calls because he's busy with his girlfriend and his son in the bedroom and he left his phone on sofa at the lounge room.

She becomes so scared, and she notices that he's busy cheating.

She sighs.

"Sometimes love become one's worst enemy in life."

She yells at Angel while Angel's busy playing game on her mother's phone in the kitchen.

"Angel!!" Elisha.

"Yes mom!" Angel.

"Bring me my phone and get yourself busy with your books!"

"Mom please!"

"I will get a stick and beat you for being ignorant on your schoolwork!"

"Don't mom! But I know everything that my teacher taught us!"

"I know you're a genius, but you need to stay focused and have self-discipline and commit yourself on schoolwork."

"Okay!"

She brings back the phone to her mother and walks to the study room.

Elisha's deeply hurt about her husband. She tries to ignore it and goes to the bedroom to take a nap.

In the morning Elisha wakes up and prepare for work; she emphatically prepares Angel for school. She did as usual firstly accompany Angel to school after that she drives to work. She's possessed by ire on her heart which makes her cry while she's driving to her work.

She arrives to work and Jessica nips striding to her. Jessica's a white nurse with pump body shape and long brown hair; she's always wearing her eyeglasses because she's opaque without glasses. She's been having a crush on Terry for a very long time, and whenever Terry comes to the hospital, she tries to get closer to him.

"Hi Mrs. Denson." Jessica.

"Hi! Jessica, how are you doing?" Elisha

"I'm doing fine, and I hope your relative's doing fine with her newborn baby."

"Which baby?"

"Oh! Sorry! Maybe she's a friend of your husband because he was here yesterday day to pick up a woman and a baby."

"What? Terry? You mean my husband?" She seems confused

"Yes!"

Elisha sighs.

"Maybe you just had some optical illusion problem! I don't think my husband indulge in making friend with women."

"I'm telling you the truth! He was here yesterday."

"You know what, am I resenting you?"

"What,                                            why?"

"You always blab like a teenager!"

"Oh! Sorry! Maybe someone in the maternity wards will tell you all about it!"

"It seems like it's something serious"

"He was here to pick up some woman with an infant! Do you think I would just lie to you? What for Elisha? What for…..?"

Elisha nipping inside the casualty realizing that Terry didn't come back home last night. She becomes meditate about it, but she didn't find an answer and a solution rather she gets a heart break. Jessica follows her trying to convince her.

"Maybe I know! Just give me some space to be alone Jessica."

"Ok, doctor-Denson!"

Elisha seems heart broken and terrified by what Jessica told her.

She shambles to the old hospital storeroom with tears in her eyes.

Doctor-Richie sees her, and he realizes that Elisha's not okay. He follows her to the storeroom and finds her glooming and sobbing inside the storeroom. He goes adjacent her and hugs her.

"What's your problem Elisha!"

"It's fine Richie, you can't solve this…."

"Maybe I can…"

"No Richie, you can't." She sobs and trudge near Richie swaying all over the storeroom.

Richie goes closer to Elisha.

"I see you're stolid, but if you trying to be stoical and never reveal what's bothering you to anyone; I'm telling you, this pain is going to give you a stroke."

"I can't continue living like this. That man is eager to tormenting me."

Richie puts Elisha in his arms again.

"It will be okay!"

Jessica follows Elisha to the storeroom to figure out if she's okay or not. But when she gets near the storeroom door, she finds Elisha and Richie hugging. She seems shocked and waits to see what will happen.

"I lost my vital life; Terry's vulgar with no respect to his woman." She says this with her head on Richie's chest.

"It will be okay!"

Richie becomes vehement to Elisha; his dick becomes harder while he still hugging Elisha; Elisha feels Richie dick on her thigh touching her, but she ignores it because she's crying and emotional. Richie slowly moves his right hand to Elisha's ass while the other hand holds Elisha tightly. He seduces her by his hand, touching her allover her body; She raises her head and look at

Richie's face but she's a little bit bashful. They start kissing and romancing each other while their hearts begin to beat faster. Richie starts touching Elisha's boobs smoothly while his other hand goes inside Elisha's pants.

Jessica is busy taking a video of Elisha and Richie while they are busy in the storeroom.

Elisha feels that Richie has already made her cookie become sock. She's panting while she holds Richie tight, and she quickly unzips his trouser. He puts her on the desk, and they start to copulate. Elisha cum and she feels so relished when she is having sex with Richie.

Jessica notices that they're finishing copulating and she quickly saves that video of Elisha and Richie, and she strays back seeming very confused.

Richie feels stupendous after he had sex with Elisha while Elisha feels a little bit abash and timid. She dresses herself up when she's sullen and she is striding back to work without talking to Richie.

She detests herself and sees herself like she's scoundrel toward her husband. But deep down inside she's proudly delight that she is enjoying Richie more than her husband Terry. Jessica peep

dingy at Elisha; she shows a great tedious toward
Elisha while Elisha smile at her

# Chapter 13

Terry is trying to be vigorous but it's seeming so difficulty for him to tell her wife Elisha that he has a son with Monica. He doesn't have any idea how he can approach his wife regarding his issue with Monica. He arranges to meet up with Simon at the beach. Terry drives to the beach and finds Simon there sitting on a camp chair drinking sherry wine using tumbler glass looking at girls wearing bikinis enjoying themselves, swimming and turbulent inside the water. Terry parks his car on the parking area and waddling where Simon's sitting. He's handling a camp chair on his right hand. It's sandy all over the beach which makes all people having turbulent movement when they walk.

"Man!" Terry

"Hey man! You have finally arrived" Simon says this while he's smiling and looking at Terry.

"Yah man" Terry

"Take a sip of sherry wine man!" Simon

"Thanks, my man!" Terry

"I'm just entertaining my eyes by looking at those girls man!" Simon

 They both laugh.

"I want to get myself a wife man!" Simon laughs.

"Yah, you need to get someone who will bear you babies and stop living this life of being a bachelor." He laughs.

 "Man, I need Sabrina with all my heart."

"Who's Sabrina?"

"That girl who's standing yonder; She's a TV presenter and story actor!"

"Sabrina?        Is        she        around        here?"

"Man! She's here, look yonder?"

"I see her now, Mm, my man! That girl's a rose! She's so charming, I mean she's beautiful."

"Hey! Hey, watch it, I know you! She's mine."

They laugh.

Yeah man, get that girl!" He points towards Sabrina. "Look how beautiful she is."

"Let me give her some time with her friends, I'II be in touch with her soon."

Terry and Simon stare at Sabrina seeming vivacious and fascinated about Sabrina. Sabrina smiles when she notices that Terry and Simon are staring at her in a seductively and sentimental way.

 Sabrina's a beautiful black slender woman with a figure body shape. She has black hair with sparkling cunning eyes. She's a TV presenter and stories actor. She got divorced by her boyfriend because he was always trying to get involve in Sabrina acting career and compel her to resign because he didn't want her to be an actress anymore from the day, he found out that she was having romantic scenes with Michael on TV. He was also controlling and always indulge himself in Sabrina's business. So, Sabrina was always nervous about his attitude; she decided to leave him and live her life alone. She has been alone for about a year now.

"So, My man! How are you coping with your life?" Simon

"Mmmm! I have made a huge mess; my ass is on fire. I'm not conceit about what I did to Elisha." Terry

 "You can't conceal what's already happen man! You need to tell her the truth!"

"Do you think she will just accept it and forgive me for what I did?"

"There is only one way to find out, just try talking to her."

"She will dump me or rather kill me!"

"How long do you think you can live with this secret?"

"Man! Don't ask that! How can I go in front of my wife and say, 'my wife I did a huge mistake, I impregnated another woman, now I'm having a son with that woman,' Do you think she will just say 'Oh! Okay it is fine let forget it and carry on with our life', do you…?"

"Maybe, who knows?" He sniggers.

 "Man stop playing!"

"I know it's awkward, but you can't live with this huge secret, if you don't tell her she will excavating this issue between you and Monica by herself! And remember if she finds out….! You're causing a blaster that is going to blow you away."

"I only want to save my marriage with Elisha."

Then, save it with the truth. Man up!"

"How?"

"You know your wife better than anyone else! Go and face her."

"I don't have any idea on how to fix this mess! I'm just left with contrite thought which is stressing my mind."

"Hold her hands and say you have a huge problem that you want to share with her."

"And then?"

"Extravagant your time with her, and when you see her becoming hysteria calm her down and say, 'I wish that we can share those enthusiasm times for the rest of our life; but for now I think this is the end for us."

"Man, stop being imprudence!"

"I'm telling you; she will become stolid and shocked. Then you will tell her what you have done. I know she will be so angry but if she totally loves you, she will never leave you."

"Ok, I will try; I wish it will be prodigy to save my relationship."

"She will allege herself for not spending time with you and not giving you sex."

"I will try man"

Simon peer to Sabrina while Terry is penitent about perpetual persecute his wife, Elisha.

Simon summons Sabrina while he seems vivacious and vigorous. Sabrina wanders from her companion and shambling to where Simon and terry are sitting. She looks so sensational and keen while she's treading to Simon.

"Hi! Mr. Denson" Sabrina

"Hey Sabrina" Terry

"Sabrina! Who summoned you?" Simon asked Sabrina.

"It's you!" She smiles and sumptuous to Simon

"Why don't you greet the one who summoned you first?" He smiles

"Ahh! I figured that we would have plenty of time, that's why I firstly greeted Mr. Denson." She smiles and shows that she's making a plea to Simon.

"Terry! Can you give us some space because there is something I'd like to discuss with Sabrina in private?" Simon

Terry and Sabrina both laugh loudly.

"Oh! Jealousy" Sabrina

Terry strays from Simon and Sabrina and shambles to Sabrina's friends. He takes off his clothes and gets in the water where Sabrina's friends are.

"Come and swim with me ladies!" Terry

They go to him and have so much fun swimming with Terry.

Simon seems terrified when he leaves with Sabrina, he is just looking at her and blah like a lunatic because his heart gets timid when he tries to say a word to Sabrina, Sabrina's looking at him while she smiles. He solicited her to ride with him when the day gets somber and when she's ready to go home.

When the day gets somber Sabrina comes to Simon so that he may accompany her home. They ride together in Simon's car. They both seem to be having a great journey since Simon is busy making a lot of teasing. Sabrina's laughing loudly as she loves jokes passionately.

Simon becomes silent and looks at Sabrina on her face while he's driving.

"What?" Sabrina seems confused

"Huh?" Simon

"Why are you looking at me like that?"

"You're so beautiful Sabrina."

"Wow! Thank you!"

"I'm having a compulsion that I can't live without you; my heart can't wait to share the unconditionally extremely devotion with your heart, I beg you to be part of everything that belongs to my life."

"I know and I could see judging be the expression on your face when you summoned me at the beach, but Simon you may not be satisfied by the way I am……"

"What do you mean?"

"Our relationship will be indomitable because it's awkward for us as celebrities to get marriage since you may end up getting jealous when you see me having another romantic relationship on TV."

"Oh! As an intellectual man, I can't be jealous by delusional things that deceive our minds and our eyes. Acting is no real, I totally understand that"

"If you promise me that you will abstain from controlling me and not induce me to abdicate to be an actress and not getting involved in my actress career."

"I love you Sabrina and I love the way you are and everything that you have. I don't think love is there to pull someone down. Please stay in my heart because that's all I want from you."

"Okay! Let me give us a chance……!"

"Thanks Sabrina, you rescued my heart, now I can be in love again."

"You're polite Simon! I deserve to be yours and I thought you're worthy to take all of me! It makes me indoctrinate when I heard the word 'love coming from your mouth."

Simon seems so blissful, and he stops his car at the site of the road. He looks at Sabrina and sigh.

He gets closer to Sabrina and place his palm on Sabrina's cheek.

"I never thought I will progress in being in love with illustrious pretty woman like you." Simon says this while showing a sad face.

"You're my sweetest devotion! I'll never regret anything while I'm adhesive next to you. I'll love you internally and never let you be far away from me!" Sabrina

"It's adventitious to get a sensational brilliant lady like you Sabrina."

"I'm all yours now Simon! I will always lay by your side for my entire life."

Sabrina smiles and gets adjacent to Simon and kisses him passionately. They get into some endless kissing inside the car. Simon adjusts Sabrina's seat so that he may kiss her avidly.

# Chapter 14

Terry seems uncertain about where he may go between Elisha and Monica's house. He realizes that Elisha will be angry with him, and he doesn't want to be in fray when he was in a zealous moment with bikinis girls at the beach. He drives to Monica's house and finds Monica busy playing with her child, He joins her, and he sits on the sofa, he kisses Monica and his baby on the forehead and gives a great smile to Monica. Elisha seems to be fighting herself to become sedate while she's siting on the couch in the lounge room. She's thinking about Richie and everything they did at the Hospital. She becomes erotic when she relives about the moment when she was having sex with Richie at the hospital. She becomes envy to be with him in this night. She sends a callback to him to test him if he may respond with call.

When Richie saw a callback from Elisha, he immediately calls her, but he feels bashful and inglorious when he's waiting for Elisha to pick up her phone.

"Hey! Doctor-Richie! I just want to…….!" Elisha says this in a hurry.

"Elisha! You need to calm down and try to dismiss that bedraggled fatuous idea which is in your mind! I won't tell anybody about what happened between us. I'II hushes up to anybody." Richie

"O! Okay, thanks!" She looks a little bit timid and frustrated

"So, what're you doing?" Richie

"I'm just sitting on the couch feeling so bored." Elisha

"Where's your Husband."

"He hasn't been coming home from last week."

"Is he busy with work?"

"Who knows?"

"Are you getting convenient with your husband?"

"Ah! Richie, let's forget about my problems; how is your wife?"

"She's doing fine!"

"That's great; are you at your surgery or have you gone home already?"

"I'm home. My wife went to attend an all-night prayer, you know she's impressionable impulse in churching stuff."

"Okay!" She sighs and becomes silent for short period of time.

"So, what's keeping you busy now?"

Richie perceives that Elisha's trying to hook up but he's pretending as if he doesn't know that she's tricking him.

"Nothing; I'm just watching comedy."

"Why don't you come over to my place?"

"Oh! I thought you didn't want to do it again?"

"Do what?" She smiles

"To have sex with me"

"Oh! I just thought that perhaps we may keep each other company, but it's fine, you can keep on watching comedy, I understand."

"Oh! I'm coming right now; I mean I too would like some company!"

Richie takes his car keys and run to his car and drives faster to Elisha's home. When he arrives at Denson's house, he finds Elisha sitting on the sofa drinking a sherry wine, she's already getting drunk.

She gives him a glass to pour himself some sherry wine for himself. They drink a lot and they both become drunk. They have a good time together drinking and dancing to the song of Whitney Houston 'Until you come back.'

 They start kissing and romancing each other while they're still drinking sherry wine mixed with Red bull and Johnny walker wine. They commit themselves to having sex in the lounge room; after that they slumber in the lounge room.


Gloria rides back home in the morning and she finds out that Richie is not at home. She becomes so perturbing about Richie.

"What's going on here?" She strides to the kid's room and find's her kids still sleeping on the bed.

She's trying to be philosophical, but it seems like it's hard for her because her heart is wreath with stoical towards Richie's actions. She's overthinking that her husband may have had an emergency at the surgery; she preoccupied a lot about Richie that makes her inhibition and feels listless.

She intends to call him, but Richie isn't picking up his phone because he is still sleeping droning in the lounge room with his other hand on Elisha's breast.

She calls him several times. Elisha she's frustrated by Richie's droning which wakes her up. She hears Richie's phone ringing, and she wakes him up.

"Richie! Your phone is ringing!"

Richie finds out that it's Gloria who's been calling, he ignores it and goes back to sleep.

"Hey! Richie! Richie! You need to get up and go before someone recognizes that you slept here! Wake up Richie!"

Richie wakes up.

"You must go now Richie!"

"Where's my car keys"

"You misplaced them?"

Richie seems to be avoiding the issue of going back home because he still needs to spend some time with Elisha; but Elisha quickly impels him to go.

Eventually Terry calls Elisha to tell her that Simon's pleading to throw a harmonious celebration for his new relationship with Sabrina at their house today. Elisha just plausible but seems ponderous about Terry's bad morals. But when Elisha heard Terry's voice, she got some feeling in her heart that compelled her that she still has a compulsion of loving him.

"Where are you, Terry?" She says this sadly and perturbing about the tormenting that Terry brings to her life. She's so stumble toward Terry.

"I was descendant to Italy for some of auditions with my group, but the problem was that I lost my phone, so I had to do a sim swap."

"Are you trying to continuously lie to me?"

"No, my love; I will be back today; and don't forget to invite your companion and your colleagues to support Simon on his celebration.

"Okay! I'II be waiting for you until you come back home." She says this while she's tedious and feeling so contrite about fornicating with Richie.

She snaps and takes a broom and begins to clean the whole lounge room to make it look tidy, she takes some perfumes, and she sprays all over the lounge for a good scent. She finishes cleaning and repose on the sofa focusing on inviting her friends and colleagues to come to Simon's celebration. She even calls Richie to invite him as well for Simon's gala dinner. But Simon had already invited Richie to come to the Denson's house for his gala and he told him to come with his wife Gloria.

Simon arrives at the Denson's house with his girlfriend Sabrina, they seem so sensational and keen.

They find Elisha laying on the sofa seeming so listless and exhausted.

"Hey! Elisha!" Simon

"Hi Simon" Elisha

"Why are you seeming so wretched and reluctant?" She smiles. "Oh! No Simon! I'm just exhausted!"

"Stop being exhausted, today is our great day to enjoy the beginning of our everlasting devotion journey." He laughs widely.

"I know! I know and we'll have a great time, I can assure you." She said that yelling joyfully.

Sabrina goes to Elisha and gives her a hand to greet her.

"Hi! I'm Sabrina!" Sabrina

"Sabrina?" Elisha

"Yes"

"Wait a minute! Simon! Are you in love with this celebrity girl?" Elisha

"Yeah; she's mine!" He smiles while he hugs Sabrina

"Wow! She's such a superb and highbrow girl! I love this girl with all my heart." Elisha

"Oh!" Sabrina gets so delightful and peaceful in her heart. "Thank you so much."

"Come let's get to know each other girl" Elisha

They hug each other passionately and Elisha gives Sabrina a baby kiss after she hugged her.

"Thank you for welcoming my girlfriend in this brilliant way Elisha! You're a nice woman indeed!" Simon

"Ah! Shut up! Let's go prepare the food Sabrina and leave this gentleman watching TV!" Elisha

"Okay!" She smiles and they both walk to the kitchen. "You're a ravishing young woman!" Sabrina

"Thanks" She smiles.

"You never told me your name since we were talking a lot, but Simon told me that you're……

"I'm Elisha!" She smiles.

"Oh! Such a nice name"

"Wear this apron so that we can prepare the best food these people have ever had."

They both laugh and they keep themselves busy with cooking and having a lot of fun together.

Terry, Eva, and Jessica arrive together. They enter the house and find Simon sitting on the sofa watching TV, Terry expresses the bashful face when entering inside the house.

"Hey! My man! Why are you taking so behindhand?" Simon says this seeming so happy

"I was busy with work man! Where's my wife?" Terry

"She's cooking with mine in the kitchen." He smiles.

"Hey! Simon! I want to meet that beautiful celebrity woman immediately!" Eva

"She's in the kitchen! You guys should go and join them!" Simon

"The two of you better go to the kitchen! We want to gossip as a man!"

"Okay! Let go Jessica!"

It seems so ponderous for Jessica to get away from Terry, but she impels herself to go with Eva to the kitchen.

"Hey! My man! I'm feeling so bashful to meet my wife!" Terry

"Try to be philosophical and go greet your wife man!" Simon

"A lot has been ruined in my marriage man!"

"You still have power to fix what's broken in your marriage!"

"Man, it can't be fixed!"

"Why?"

"I have a baby with Monica!"

"What the hell! What're you talking about…? How….? I mean….. You were serious when you told me that you impregnated her?"

"You need to hush up about this because Elisha doesn't know about this."

"Oh! Shit..! Man! What have you done?"

"Let's just drop this topic! We'II talk about it later."

Richie and his wife arrive at the Denson's house. Simon and Terry seem so keen when they see Richie arriving to the celebration.

"Hey! Richie! I thought that you weren't going to make it since you are always a busy man!" Terry says this while he's smiling

"Ah! I just had to manage time so that I'd be here to help my cousin celebrate his new love!"

"That's great my man! Take a seat."

Terry and Simon stand up to greet Gloria passionately.

Elisha and her colleagues and her companions finished cooking and goes back to the lounge room. When Elisha finds Terry, Simon and Richie having an impressionable fun conversation, she becomes inhuman and resentful. She goes back to the kitchen seeming inhibition and she's swaying all over the kitchen. Terry follows her to the kitchen.

"Hi! My wife" Terry seems cautious

She swivels and looks at Terry with a shy face, she seems like she doesn't have any idea how she will respond to him.

"I know I have done a reprehensibly mistake but I'm repenting on that." He also says this with a shy face towards Elisha.

"Don't even say that! You made me look like trash; I did something that ignominious my reputation because you were abandoning me!" Elisha yelling at Terry while she's sobbing.

"I know this is my fault entirely, but please I'm contrite about that, you don't deserve to be tormented."

"I don't deserve you, Terry!" She says this while she's still sobbing

"I know, but we can fix this and rehabilitate our marriage."

"This is your fault, Terry! You left me home alone without telling me where you are going! Now I'm ignominious because of repulsiveness that you did towards me! You don't care about me Terry! You don't care….!" She cries and Terry goes to her and hugs her.

"It will be okay my love!" He wipes her tears off with his jacket.

"I love you Terry" Elisha says this while wiping her tear with a towel.

"I love you too Elisha!" He seems suspicious.

"Promise me you'll never abandon me again"

"Let's go to lounge room and have a good moment with others."

They hold each other by hands and goes to the lounge room where other people are settling. Elisha feeling retiring when she looks at Richie. But she tries to avoid it and focusing on having fun with her husband Terry. But it's ponderous to Richie to see Elisha and Terry having much romantic fun at that trice.

Simon gets up from the sofa and go to the radio to select a song, he selects the song called 'And I'm Telling You I'm Am Not Going' by Jennifer Hudson. They all get so sensational by that song and they started dancing with their partners.

Richie got monotonous and jealousy when he sees Terry dancing with his wife Elisha griping her by her waist and kissing her on her neck.

Gloria peep at Richie and notice that he may be feeling bored, she gets up with a smile and hold Richie by his hands.

"Come and dance with me my love."

He seems so cautious, but he immediately ignores Elisha, and he gets up and dance with his wife Gloria.

"You're integral to my life Elisha, I really miss you!" Terry says this and kisses Elisha on her lips while wriggling and dancing with her.

Elisha's smiling whiles she's holding Terry on his shoulder. She's looking so zealous when she is having her husband Terry on her site.

Richie peeps at Elisha dingily and Elisha peeps back at Richie confusingly, she becomes so tedious by the way Richie's focusing and concentrating on her.

Simon and his girlfriend Sabrina are dancing passionately. The song that's playing changed to, 'Cry No More-By Charlie Wilson.

Simon kneels and takes out a ring from his pocket while he stares Sabrina on her face, he shows a shy face toward Sabrina.

Elisha sees that Simon's kneeling down and she shrieking to people to be noiseless and focus on Simon and Sabrina, she suddenly puts the radio on mute.

"Sabrina!" Simon

Sabrina's just looking at him seeming shocked.

"Yes" Sabrina

"Will you marry me?" Simon becomes fulfilling with terror.

She's just quiet and immediately becomes prude, most people feel sympathies towards Simon, in their hearts they feel a little bit frightened and they're flouncing by the way Sabrina hesitates to answer. Elisha looks at Sabrina and node her head.

"Yes! I will marry you!" She says this and put her palm on Simon's head.

Simon takes a deep breath and puts a ring on Sabrina's finger.

Everyone seems so happy for Simon's proposal. Elisha leaves Terry and goes to dance with Simon, she was so happy and sensational for Simon and Sabrina.

Terry smiles and take Sabrina and kisses her in her hand and dance with her.

**Chapter 15**

Elisha seems meekest towards her husband Terry after Simon's proposal. She knows deeply that she treacherous Terry by having fornication with Richie several times.

She's trying so hard to initiate her relationship for rehabilitation so that it may be back to normal and keenness. She doesn't want anything to do with Richie anymore since she wants to rebuild her marriage.

Jessica's going up and down at the hospital searching for Eva. She finds her outside siting on a chair chatting with Elisha on her phone. Elisha took a day off because she's not feeling well.

"Hey! Eva! I was searching for you all over the hospital!"

"Why?" She looks confused

"I have a lot on my mind, and I think it would be best if I share it with you. It's about your friend!"

"Oh! Please Jessica my friend's business doesn't concern me, I can only assist by given you her digits then you may call her!"

"No....! I just want to show you something! Or I can send it to you via whatsApp." Jessica says this cautiously

She instantaneous sends that video of Richie having fornication with Elisha to Eva.

"I have already sent you the video." Jessica

"Let me check it. But what's this video all about?" Eva

"Look at it" Jessica

She views it and realizes that it is a sex tape.

"What the hell? This is an abomination, Jessica! Are you sending me pornography?" She becomes furious when she hears erotic sounds.

"No! This is not pornography; it's a sex tape of Richie and Elisha!"

"What…?" She views the video again and she perceives it's Richie and Elisha having sex at the hospital storeroom; she seems outrange and confused. "Tell me, am I having an optical illusion?"

"This is going to be impudent to your friend."

"I know! I'm just cautious now….! But why don't we try to make this stay between us?"

"It's inevitable for now because so many people have already seen this video!"

"I know but delete that video! This video is going to make Elisha's life indomitable! It's going to ruin her career!"

"Okay I will delete it but as I said, a lot of people have seen that sex tape."

"Mmh! What the hell did Elisha do to herself? This is an absolute disaster."

"Let me go Eva! I'II sees you tomorrow!"

"Okay..! But wait…wait…..!"

Eva tries a lot to indoctrinate Jessica to hush up to everyone.

"Don't tell anybody; do you hear me!"

"Yah; I heard you!"

Jessica gets in her car and takes off. On her way out she realizes that she must call Terry for a meet up. Terry also took a day off from work to spend his time with Elisha. Meanwhile, Terry and Elisha are lying on the bed; Terry hangs his right hand on Elisha's shoulder. He hears his phone ringing and tries to avoid it because he thought it may be a call from work. Elisha swivels her body to Terry.

"Why're you avoiding your phone? Is there something hideous that you're trying to hide from me?" Elisha

"No my love; I don't want anybody to interrupt and ruin our day!" Terry

"Take your call Terry!"

"But my love…! I don't want to go to work and leave you alone today; I just want to spend the whole day with you."

"Pick up you phone Terry, unless you are trying to hide something from me."

"Okay!" Terry gets off from the bed and go to pick up his phone.

 He notices its Jessica calling and he thought maybe she needs to talk to Elisha. He takes the call.

"Hello" (Terry answering his phone).

"Hey Terry; we need to meet immediately!"

"Why? What for..?"

"There's something I'd like to show you!"

"What's that?"

"Let's meet at special pub!"

"You should at least give me a clue on what the meeting is about"

"No, Well, This…. This has to do with your wife."

"What?" He becomes confused.

 "Come to special pub and don't tell her about the meeting."

"What the hell! Okay I'm coming now!" Terry hangs up his phone and goes to Elisha, pretending as if he was talking to Simon.

"Okay Simon! I'm on my way right now!" Terry pretending.

 He quickly takes a bath and dresses up.

"Wow! Terry, where are you going?"

"Oh! Remember the call I took earlier? That was Simon, he wanted me to help him find the best suit for the wedding, so I must go to him like yesterday!" he laughs

"Okay no problem! I also wanted to go to the surgery for some work!"

"Okay my love." He kisses her on her cheek and snip ride to the special pub with his BMW X5.

He arrives at special pub and finds Jessica drinking red wine. He greets her and gives her a kiss on her cheek.

"How are you doing Terry?" Jessica greets Terry.

"I'm fine and you?" Terry replies.

"I'm fine too. I was didn't mean to interrupt your day but there's something that I want to show you!"

"You said it's something about Elisha, right?"

"Yes"

"What's going on?"

"Well, it's about Elisha and Richie. They're fornicating." She simpers

"Ha! Don't play with my mind Jessica please! Don't…..! He seems frustrated.

"I'll shows you the video!"

"What…!"

She gives him her cellphone.

"Watch this!"

He watches her wife and Richie having sex at the hospital storeroom.

"What the………!" He seems so frustrated and he idiosyncrasy like a lunatic person, but he tries to be philosophical when he sees that Jessica's prude by his action.

"Send me that video now!" He yells at Jessica.

Jessica sends the video immediately to Terry's via WhatsApp. She seems so frightened.

 He gets out of the pub and tread near his car. He stares at the sky, and he takes a deep breath; He gets inside the car and drives to Monica's house. He's so exasperated by Elisha. His face changes, looking creepy. He arrives at Monica's house seeming so disappointed. Monica nips to him seeming so confused by the way Terry looks.

"Why're you looking so disappointed and ire?" Monica

"Watch this" Terry gives his phone to Monica in a gawk way.

Monica watches the sex tape of Richie and Elisha and smiles.

Terry goes straight to bedroom and takes his gun and put it on his waist, he comes back to the lounge room and finds Monica still watching that sex tape.

He deprives his phone from Monica and hurries to his car. He's so pugnacious and he gets in the car.

"Don't do something stupid Terry!" She said that and immediately gets inside the house. She sighs and takes her phone from the sofa. She thought of sending some photos of herself with Terry and her son to Elisha, she sends that photo to Elisha via WhatsApp. Elisha's busy at her dignitary office writing some prescriptions for a patient. She hears a message alert from her phone, she picks it up and views the photo. Elisha becomes muddled and eager to call that number which sent her the photo. She immediately calls that number.

"Hey! Who's that?" She said that angrily.

"It's Monica! I'm the mother of Terry's son!"

"What..?"

"We were together that day at the park. Do you still remember the pregnant woman? That was me, I was impregnated by your husband Terry."

Elisha becomes sullen glooming and feeling reluctant to talk too much because she's shocked and jumbled and becomes feeble with what Monica just said to her about her husband.

"And one other thing, Terry bought us a big, ravishing house at the suburb, Mk Street. He always spends his time with me and the baby!"
Elisha's just listening to Monica while she's busy slandering her. She hangs up and cries.

Terry calls his friend Simon while he was on the way
"Hey! My man! What's up?" Simon
"Hey! Where're you?" Terry asks Simon
"I'm at Richie's Garden!"
"Oh! so; Can you help me with something at my house?"
 "Okay! I can assist!"
 "Thanks man! What's Richie doing?"
"He's busy ploughing and irrigating."
"I'm pleading you to hurry up man please!"
"I'm on my way." Simon gets in his car and drives to Terry Denson's place.
Terry's puffing out a smoke of cigarette inside his car while he drives to Richie's; He's so melancholy and aggressive. He arrives at Richie's Garden and finds Richie busy ploughing; Terry seems clumsy and aggressive when he sees Richie. He gets to where Richie is and pulls out a gun.

"Hi Richie; How are you doing?" Terry

Richie swivels to the Terry when he gets towards him.

"I'm good! Oh, Terry! What're you doing her? I thought it was you calling Simon, he just left not so long ago, heading to your place"

"Yeah, it was me!"

"He's already gone to your place!" Richie said that seeming a bit scared

"I came for you!" He said that while he seems pugnacious.

"Ok" He sighs. "Then; what do you want?"

Terry looks at Richie dingy.

"Oh Richie….! You thought my wife's cookie is so delicious than any women you were sleep with, right?"

"Man, please I don't know what you're talking about" He seems inglorious and quail

"I'm talking about my wife's cookie man; she's so good in bed, right? I know! I know my wife when it comes to copulating, she's so good and tactics to grasp the man's desire."

"Man; I don't have any idea on what you're talking about."

Terry walks towards Richie and punch him on his cheek.

"Don't take me like a lunacy; do you think you can fool me?"

Richie become so nerves and aggressive, he belligerent himself with Terry. He punches Terry on his chin and Terry falls. He quickly goes to Terry and gives him another punch on his face and runs to take a hoe to beat Terry. Terry takes out his gun and shoots Richie on his back three times, he sees that Richie has fallen then he strides faster to his car. He gets inside his car and drives home. He finds Simon waiting for him, he greets him when he's still inside the car.

"Man; where have you been?" Simon

"Ah! Man, you're late; someone already helped me with that matter. I was accompanying him to his apartment." Terry said that seeming shocked and cautious.

"Okay no problem! May I go back home?" Simon

"Yah go man!"

"Okay!" He gets in his car. "I want to pass through Richie's Garden to takes some vegetables."

"Okay man! What……?" He seems confused.

## Chapter 16

Elisha's ponder and eliciting a lot about why her husband ponderous her in such a way of putting her in wretched and melancholy. She's so furious and crying while her heart possesses with ire. She takes her phone and calls Eva.

"Eva!" Elisha

 "Yeah Elisha" She's trying to trifle her since she saw her fornicating with Richie

"I want you to do me a favor."

"What kind of favor?"

"I found out that Terry was fornicating with that girl whom we spent time with her that day at the

park. She was impregnated by my husband Terry, now they have a son together!"
"What the hell?" Eva
"Calm down! I want you and hurry up and look for Monica's file and finds out who's the father of her child."
Eva immediately goes to look for Monica's file
"Okay!  I'm on it! But you shocked me by your stupid actions Elisha! Why did you fornicate with Richie?" Eva
"This is not the suitable time to judge each other and point fingers; I need you on my side more than ever, you are my best friend for Christ's sake."
"Oh! Shit" she says this while she holds Monica's file.
"What?"
"The father of Monica's child is Terry Denson."
"Shit; I knew it; this man was treacherous behind my back to ruin my life."
"This is precisely extraordinary in your marriage!" Eva said that seeming devastated.
Simon goes back to the Richie's Garden, and he finds Richie deceased with three bullets holes on his back, laying on the ground.  He immediately calls Elisha.

"Hold on Eva, Simon's calling me!" Elisha.

"Ok no problem." Eva.

She takes the call from Simon.

"Elisha! Elisha…..!" He said that on the phone full of shock

"Hello Simon!" Elisha

"Richie is dead! I found his deceased body at his garden now!! He's dead!" He says this oblique while he's sobbing.

"What the hell...!"

Simon hangs up his phone call with Elisha and he immediately calls the police. He's so devastated. Elisha calls Eva again.

"Richie is dead!" Elisha says this sobbing.

"What…?" Eva seems shocked.

"He got shot on his back three times."

"What the hell?"

"It's Terry! It's Terry; I know, it's him!" Elisha seems exasperating by Terry, and she seems so angry at him.

"Please my friend! You can't live with that horrible man anymore! You need to hurry up and take Angel from school and leave that house as soon as possible."

"Let me hurry up before something terrible happens to my baby." She compiles her things and put them inside her bag and nips to her car. She drives to Angel's school and finds her playing with her school companions. She summons her and Angel nip to her mother's car, she enters inside the car and Elisha greets her then she accelerates car to her home. She's gets home in time and her fear were subsided after she took her daughter from school.

She opens the door and enters inside the house with her daughter Angel.

She hears the car hoot outside and she perceives that it must be Terry. Terry notices that Elisha's indoor, he puts his gun on his waist and enters the house. He finds Elisha frightened in the middle of the lounge room.

Angel is fascinated when she sees her father because it's has been a while without seeing him.

"Daddy" She's smiling at her father, but Terry looks at her dingy.

Angel notices that there's something wrong with her father. She grabs her mother tightly while she's filled with terror. Her heart is pounding like a drum at a rockstar's concert.

Terry thrashes to Elisha.

"Do you think you can get away with this mess? You betrayed me!" Terry says this with tears in his eyes.

"Terry, did you kill Richie, are you the cause of his murder?" Elisha says this crying out loud like a little girl who has just lost her brand-new birthday doll.

"Don't ask me that nonsense! You were fornicating with him, right?"

"No! I I'd never do that!"

Terry takes out his phone, he opens that sex tape and shows Elisha. When Elisha sees her sex tape with Richie she starts to cry and ire.

"You're a savage Terry! You are full of shit!" She yells at Terry.

Terry's frustrated and exasperated to look at Elisha. He takes out his gun and points it at Elisha's stomach.

"My love; we can't be obstreperous by things that deceives us, we need to fix this rather than torment and scorn each other. I love you, Terry! I love you more than you think." Elisha

"Don't….! Stop fooling me! You're occasionally fornicating with your colleague, and you thought I wouldn't figure it out? Huh?" He yells at Elisha

"You're responsible for all this mess Terry! You're the one who impel me to commit myself on cheating!"

"How; what are you talking about?"

"You became oddity and vulgar towards me, you were not taking care of me anymore and not looking after me Terry!" She yells at Terry

"You were out casting me, Elisha! You were even procrastinating to extravagate your time with me! You omitted having me!" He cries.

"No Terry! No, we can…!" She cries.

"It's too late! It's behindhand!"

Elisha perceiving Terry ominous, and she becomes pessimist, she immediately hugs her daughter Angel when she realizes she's in snag.

Terry looks at Elisha while he cries deeply and seems sinister. He points his gun at Elisha's waist, and he pulls the trigger, he shoots Angel on her shoulder, and she falls. He becomes so devastated and frustrated when he notices that he just shot her daughter. He turns back and run away from his home; he runs out using the back door.

Elisha seems shocked and she becomes devilment when she looks at her daughter. She stands up and sees Angel collapse on the floor bleeding. She screams and cries and starts to shout for help. She suddenly picks her up and runs with her to her car, she lays her at the back seat of her car and drives her to the hospital. She seems so devastated when she's driving. She arrives at hospital and yells for help at casualty. Two nurses nip with a wheelchair, and they take Angel to the emergency room. Eva strides to Elisha holding a cup of coffee, she seems so confused and shattered and shivering.

"What happened Elisha?" Eva seems frustrated

"He shot her!" Elisha is sobbing but she's trying to be valiant.

"What the hell!"

"Don't get destructed! Just….! Look after my daughter and make sure she's alright!"

"She will be alright! I will try to resurrect her from that bedridden."

"I want to retaliate that bastard, he pretention that he can escape forever!"

Elisha gets inside her car and drives to a place where they sell illegal guns. She arrives at that place and sees two men staring at her. She wipes her tears with a towel and gets out of the car facing those two men, she strides towards them seeming furious.

"I know you! You're a doctor, right? You are Terry Denson's wife" Erick says this while he stares at Elisha.

"Can you assist me with a gun?" Elisha

"Gun? What do you want to do with a gun?" Erick

Elisha takes out a lot of money on her pocket and gives it to Erick.

"Give her the gun Erick!" Philip says this with a dingy look towards Elisha. "Give her what she wants Erick; what're you waiting for!"

Erick gets inside the building and comes back holding a gun and two packs of bullets and he gives them to Elisha.

"Do you want us to teach you how to shoot?" Philip

"I already know!" She swivels to her car.

 "Hey! I saw your man passing through yonder!" Erick says this to Elisha.

She swivels to Erick.

"Were?"

"He was running towards to the bridge."

"Okay! Look after my car!" She takes three steps toward the gravel-road, and she sees the bridge and a lot of trash all around the place. The place has become more of a dumping site since everybody throws garbage there. She loads three bullets on to her gun. She shambles to the bridge holding the gun with her right hand. She sees someone sitting inside the bridge seeming inactive; she runs towards the bridge.

Terry's sitting inside the bridge seeming gloomy and wondering about her daughter. He's crying and sobbing. He sees someone coming in a hurry to the bridge, but he takes it behindhand to notice that it may be Elisha. He immediately stands up and stares at Elisha.

Elisha enters inside the bridge and points a gun at Terry's head.

"Elisha!" Terry talks to her in shock, he tries to be presumptuous, but he becomes premonition when he sees that Elisha's looking so inhuman.

"Do you think you can outstrip for the rest of your life?" Elisha says this with a gun pointing at Terry's head

"Elisha! We can fix this! Don't do something trespass to me!" Terry seems timid.

Elisha becomes sob and frustrated.

"I love you Terry, but there's nothing I can do about it!" She cries and shed tears from her eyes while she looks at Terry, pointing a gun at him.

"I love you too Elisha!" He says this crying.

"Sorry Terry!" She pulls the trigger and shoots Terry on his forehead, and he falls, she goes to him and shoot him two more times on his chest. She swivels and goes back to where she had parked her car. Erick and Philip are just staring at her when they're sullen. She gets inside her car and drives back. She's accelerating her car to Monica's house. She arrives at the house and packs her car outside, she gets out of her car looks at Monica's house. She strides near the house, and she knocks on the door holding her gun.

"Who's that?" Monica yells while she's busy takes a bath.

"Open up!" Elisha yells

"Come inside!"

Elisha opens the door and enters inside the house. She finds Bonafide sitting on the sofa playing with his toys; she peeps dingy at him and goes to him and sit on the same sofa with him while she's holding gun; she brushes his hair with her hand.

"You're so handsome! Where's your mom?" Elisha talks to Bonafide while brushing his hair
Bonafide's busy focusing on playing with his toys. Monica gets out of the bathroom wearing nothing but a white towel; she goes to the lounge room and finds Elisha sitting close to her baby holding gun. She gets shocked and screams.

"You must shut up or I may blow your head off!" Elisha says this aggressively.
"Please! Don't spite my son! He's still….!"
She points the gun at Monica
"Let go back to the bathroom!"
"Okay!" She seems frightened and outrageous.
"Don't do something stupid Elisha please!" Monica
"Get inside the bathroom!" Elisha pointing the gun at Monica
Monica enters inside the bathroom seeming shocked. She swivels and looks at Elisha while she cries. Elisha stops at the bathroom while Monica stands in the middle of the bathroom.

"I'm sorry Elisha!" She cries "I'm sorry for taking your man from you! I…..! I wasn't aware"
"Do you know how much I loved my husband? Do you know where we would have been together if it weren't from you?"

"You can take him back! I'm sorry I wasn't fastidious and alert that I'm going to face these consequences! Take him back, I don't want him anymore. He is all yours!" She says this while crying.

"Unfortunately, he's already dead! I killed him!"

"You did what?"

"You turned me into a monster, and now you must pay the price …!" Elisha

"But don't….!" Monica

She points the gun at Monica's chest and shoots her twice. She goes back to the lounge room and picks up Bonafide. She looks at his face and nodes her head.

"You're a handsome boy my child!"

She walks to her car with the baby in her arms. She puts him in the front sit of the car and drives home slowly. On her way, she decides to play Lou Rawls song- 'If you got to make a fool of somebody'.

## THE END